CW00730110

Mad Scientist Journal: Autumn 2016

Edited by Dawn Vogel and
Jeremy Zimmerman

Cover Art by Ariel Alian Wilson
Cover Layout by Katie Nyborg

CONTENTS

FICTION

RESOURCES

ABOUT

ACKNOWLEDGMENTS

Many thanks to Patreon backers Simone Cooper, Wendy Wade, John Nienart, Army Vang, Andrew Cherry, Michele Ray, and Torrey Podmajersky!

LETTER FROM THE GUEST EDITOR
by Giverov Vings MD, PhD, as provided by Darci Vogel

Dear Readers,

After returning from a vacation, I am reminded of the inconvenience of travel. Airplanes, trains, and cars alike are annoyingly slow. Unlike birds, who, with their speedy wings, can fly quite steadily along at an honest rate, mankind is condemned to stay cramped in a small space for hours on end just to travel to the next state.

However, the long drive home I was forced to endure was good for something. I have a basic understanding of what it would take to give humans wings. While I am occupied with more important matters, you, fellow mad scientist, may undertake this project. Use your knowledge and skills to complete this task, and give humans the power of unassisted flight.

I will now share with you my understanding of what it will take to complete this project. For a full grown adult, you would merely weld bird wings onto their arms. In the end, though, it's just a waste of time since they would die without giving the next generation wings, and then you would have to begin again.

It's babies and young children I'm interested in. A more complex matter, you see, as you would have to splice bird wing genes with human arm genes so the wings would grow with the child. Unfortunately, which genes need to be spliced, I don't know, and figuring that out is a dangerous business. The wrong combination will most likely result in death, and humans aren't that fond of letting you experiment on their offspring. Which gene you pick is your problem, but I hope you will realize the beauty of this plan and execute it.

Good luck,
Giverov Vings

Giverov Vings is a fifty-three-year-old professional mad scientist. He made his fortune early by designing a part that was critical to the success of Cessna plane engines. After a tragic experiment on his girlfriend left him single, he moved into an underground bunker in Berlin, though where in Berlin exactly, no one knows. He now spends most of his time working on taking over the world and folding laundry.

Darci Vogel is an eleven-year-old girl who lives in Lockport, Illinois, with her younger brother and parents. When she's not learning at her school, Vine Academy, she likes to read, philosophize, dance, bike, and most importantly, write. She dreams of becoming a professional author, but for now she writes as a hobby.

ESSAYS

FINAL THOUGHTS

An essay by Joshua Harken, as provided by Aaron Moskalik

———

"I love you, man." Jericho Bailey plants his face in my chest and puts me in a bear hug.

I hold my drink out to the side, careful not to spill it. It's all too much. Jericho Freaking Bailey. And here I am in his house. Mansion?

Palatial estate.

No one had seen Jericho in a decade. The rumor is he doesn't let anyone in. Even the delivery guys have to unload half a mile up the road, and robots take it the rest of the way.

Well, there's never been a party I couldn't crash. In this case, I brought the party to Jericho. Three of my closest friends are downstairs right now, exploring his well-stocked bar.

OK, so I met them just last Tuesday, but Hell, we're on a road trip together, and by definition that makes us besties, right?

California, here we come. We cruise down the Coastal Highway where it turns inland a few miles and gets lost among the hills. Angelica ... Angelique asks, "Isn't this where that hermit billionaire lives? What wouldn't I give to see his digs."

Digs? Who talks like that? Anyway, I whip the Mustang onto the first turn off and head straight up a mountain. When we get to the top, I point toward the ocean. The sun glints off something hidden behind the palm trees. "That's where Jericho Bailey lives," I tell them. "On a clear day, you can see Hawaii from his penthouse."

"Yeah, how would you know?" Desiree ... Denise asks.

"Jericho and I are tight. We went to college together."

"Maybe you can introduce us?" Damien says. Damien is full of ideas. "Let's check out that hot ride you're always talking about.

5

Let's go on a road trip. Let's drive along the coast." Maybe it's his muscles rippling under his too tight shirt or the way his brown eyes twinkle over that crooked grin, but the girls always endorse his suggestions, and I can't help but go along.

This time I'm not so sure though. I haven't spoken to Jericho in twenty years. It was the first and last time I saw him laugh.

I call Jericho quirky, and he says, "I'm not quirky, I'm quarky," and laughs. I don't get it, but laugh along anyway. Jericho laughing is an inexplicably beautiful thing. I want him to laugh again. We drink wine and talk of many things.

"So let me get this straight. Your theory says we can get unlimited energy for free?" I ask.

"Under the right conditions, we can set up a controlled reaction." He wags his finger at me. "But, it is inherently unstable. It throws off exotic particles. Strange quarks—" he points to himself "—and charm quarks—" he points to me. "If they combine in just the right way, the resulting particles will convert any matter they come in contact with."

"Then what?"

"An exponential chain reaction. An uncontrolled release of energy." He sits down next to me. His eyes appear magnified by his glasses. His gaze is focused enough to start a fire.

I swirl my wine, avoiding his stare. "What are the odds of that happening?"

"Infinitesimal at first. Inevitable in the end." He moves closer.

I stand up. "Sounds dangerous. Desperate."

He just watches me with a sad knowing look.

The robots swarm the car as we approach Jericho's mansion. "State your business."

"Tell Jericho Josh is here to see him. Joshua Harken."

The robots go silent. Their little red lights blink at us. The barrels of their guns point at us.

Denise makes herself as small as possible in the back seat. "Maybe we should go."

As usual, Damien fiddles with his smart phone.

The largest robot beeps. Angelique shrieks.

"You are expected. Proceed." The robots clear a path, and I drive in.

Once inside, it's not long before Jericho and I ditch the others and head upstairs. Just like I imagined, the whole top floor is glass.

"So how do you know Damien?" I ask Jericho.

"You figured it out." Jericho offers me a glass of wine. "He's my chief of security."

"And he lives here. Just the two of you?" I hadn't noticed how warm the room was.

Jericho raises a brow. "I sent him away. To get you."

I sip my wine. Time to change the subject. "Did you do it? Did you build your doomsday device?" I ask.

Jericho chuckles. I'm disappointed he doesn't laugh. His hair has thinned out on top, but it's the same Jericho squinting out behind those glasses. "Was there ever any question? Why do you think everything is so cheap these days?"

He points to where the sun is preparing to dip herself into her pink bath. "We built it deep under the ocean, a thousand miles from anywhere. It powers everything now. The big boys keep its existence quiet, though. They want everyone to think it's business as usual."

"Won't you get in trouble telling me?"

Jericho shakes his head. "Watch."

It's gradual at first. I think it's just the tide going out, but the water continues to run away from us until seagulls are diving for the fish that flop exposed on the dry ocean bed.

Then the sun disappears. Not gradually. All at once. Night drops on us like a roofie washed down with whiskey.

"Here it comes," Jericho whispers.

A big black wall swallows the stars as it marches toward us.

Tsunami.

Doomsday.

Kawabunga.

It was inevitable. I know that now. I've always known, but somehow I'd managed to hide from it all these years. Now it's here, cresting over us. Jericho trembles as I wrap him in my arms. "I love you too."

Joshua Harken was living a lie. Fast cars, casual friends, it all blurred together as one big skid-mark of a life. All he knew was he had to keep the pace, or he'd realize where he went wrong.

Nobody knew how unhappy he was. His quick wit and devilish

charm made sure of that. He kept on the move anyway. No sense taking any chances. Joshua couldn't outrun his dreams though, a half-forgotten face behind Coke-bottle glasses. Get him drunk enough, he might even say his name, Jericho Bailey. Yes, that Jericho Bailey. Jericho the Freaking Billionaire Recluse Bailey.

Aaron Moskalik was supposed to be writing his doctoral dissertation. Instead, he found himself producing lexical doodles, odd scraps of poems, and pieces of stories. This compulsion subsided for the better part of a decade after graduation. Life happened, a wife, a day job, a daughter.

A few years ago he rediscovered the passion to write and decided to study the craft this time around and produce finished works that will be happily read.

TO DR. VON LUPE, CONCERNING THE ICE PICK
A letter by Dr. Elizabeth Chu, as provided by Alanna McFall

To Dr. Von Lupe, My Most Glorious God-on-Earth and Leader Among All the Ranks of Humans,

Greetings to you, my dark master who claims dominion over the land and the skies (and in whose name we are all working hard on claiming the seas). I hope that you are doing well when you receive this letter, and that the tax season was a smooth and painless one for you. You know what they say: the only entity that comes close to being as evil and powerful as the esteemed Dr. Von Lupe is the IRS. I say that all the time. As a captive in your underground lair, I have greatly appreciated not having to file my returns this year. Truly, I thank you for this gift.

However, I am writing to you today because of an issue I am currently facing that may have arisen out of your wise and omnipotent orders. To be direct and to the point and not to waste your precious time or attention, let me be brief: the lab where we are growing and teaching our hyper-intelligent squid has become a hostile work environment. And for the sake of the advancement of the dark sciences, the conditions must improve.

(I apologize, I see that my blood has begun to drip onto this page. I hope you will forgive the mess, as we are short on writing materials.)

Before anything else, let me be clear about two points: firstly, my colleague Dr. Kimberly Quinn is a gifted scientist and a talented woman in many regards. Secondly, if there is ever a question of which one of us your esteemed gaze should find disposable, you should exterminate her immediately and retain me as your loyal servant. These opinions may seem contradictory, but I believe that my balance of admiration and pragmatism has allowed me to form a rounded and honest opinion of my fellow captive. Though we come from very different walks of life out in the free world that I can scarcely remember anymore, and although I have over twenty years of seniority on her, I have come to consider us friends. And when kept in extreme isolation with only cephalopods and the occasional soldiers in your Shadow Army to talk to, a good friend can be essential.

So with all this in mind, you can see how I would be quick to notice changes in her behavior, as has come to pass over the past two months. Dr. Quinn has become noticeably tense and jumpy in her daily work, far more than her usual level of anxiety, and she does not appear to sleep anymore. Ever. Unless she has taken to falling asleep moments after I do and awakening seconds before I arise, I have seen no evidence of her sleeping in the last two weeks. I am well aware, my king of the shadows and the void, that you consider sleep a sign of weakness and claim to have never indulged in it. But for fragile peons such as Dr. Quinn and me, it is an important consideration and a prerequisite for effective research and clinical work.

You may now be asking your terrifying self why I am bothering you with the personal matters of a lowly scientist. But I must confess that I do not believe Dr. Quinn's issues have sprung entirely from the depths of her own mind. Indeed, when I investigated her side of our designated sleeping hovel, I discovered something of great interest. Tucked into a crack in the sheer stone walls, obscured by a patch of moss and general cave slime (which I have come to enjoy the aesthetics of and do not complain about at all), was a miniscule transmitting device. When I listened to it carefully, I found that it produced a small, high-pitched tone that seemed to waver and warble as I listened. Holding it to my ear for even a few moments seemed to produce a feeling of vague anxiety within me. I can hardly imagine what it must have been like for Dr. Quinn to sleep near such a device.

Again, you may ask, why do I bring this to your attention? Psychological attacks cannot be a rare tactic amongst the foolish throngs who seek to un-throne you. However, given that under closer investigation, the device carried a microscopic etching, an attractive and decorative label reading "Property of Dr. Von Lupe, Forever May His Dark Reign Preside," I began to feel the sneaking suspicion that Dr. Quinn's afflictions may be somehow connected to you.

I am not saying that you cannot perform psychological experiments on your captives; I am well aware that that would be overstepping my bounds, my liege, as well as just being rude in general. But I do question the utility of using one of your brilliant scientists as a test subject. It must be said that, in general, researchers subjected to torture and extreme sleep deprivation do not tend to successfully breed enormous and sentient squid.

Dr. Quinn's increasingly erratic behavior has created an atmosphere of tension, not a fertile soil for science to spring forth from. Our prize subject, the squid named Suzie Q, has been very disturbed by the changes in one of her maternal figures. I am also dismayed at the occasional violence that Dr. Quinn has directed towards me. If my handwriting appears different in this letter, it is because I have had to write it with my left hand; there is currently an ice pick buried in my right shoulder, and it is severely impeding my ability to work. This inconvenience, and the fact that I had to restrain Dr. Quinn using several of the scarves that the squid have crocheted, should make it clear that the current status quo cannot stand within this cave.

Also, I would appreciate a visit from a doctor, if it is at all feasible.

My overlord and god of the starless nights, I understand that a large part of your overall plan's mission statement is a dedication to evil above all else. But there must be a point where evil gives way to pragmatism. And when you are conducting seemingly random tests upon otherwise useful minions for no readily apparent reason, depriving an ongoing research project of one and a half scientists, I fear you might have to take a step back and question how close you are to that line. Though it now occurs to me that your intentions might simply be too obscure for my lowly mind, and that I might in fact be a control subject in a more methodical test than I can see. If that is indeed the case, I will confess both my displeasure and my understanding.

In any case, I hope that you will take my words into consideration. For the time being, I have destroyed the transmitting device. If one is to reappear in our sleeping crag, I will take it as a sign that you disagree with my feelings on this matter, and I thank you for your consideration regardless.

I see now that my blood has begun to stain this paper more than is acceptable, so I will draw my letter to a hasty close before I lose consciousness. Send my best regards to Mrs. Von Lupe and little Julia, and congratulations on the news that you and your wife are expecting another girl. Julia must be so excited to be a big sister to another foul princess presiding over the plains of the wretched. Dr. Quinn would send her own regards, but she is otherwise occupied trying to chew through one of the scarves. I am sure she sends her best, flawed as that may be at the moment.

Sincerely,
Your Wounded but Eternally Loyal Vassal,
Dr. Elizabeth Chu

Breaking news on the disappearance of marine biologist Dr. Elizabeth Chu, who vanished nearly one year ago during a vacation near the Ural Mountains: authorities say that there is a possible link between the disappearance of Dr. Chu and the activities of a new terrorist cell working out of the mountain region. What use this shadowy group would have with one of the world's leading experts in cephalopod biology has yet to be discovered, but police are hot on the trail of the kidnappers. Any leads pertaining to the location of Dr. Chu should be brought to the appropriate authorities immediately.

Alanna McFall is an upcoming science fiction and fantasy writer. She has worked in a variety of mediums, from short stories to novels to audio scripts, and across a range of locations, stretching the span of the country from New York to Minnesota to California. She is always looking for ways to expand her repertoire and get involved in her next project. Follow her work on Twitter at @AlannaMcFall, or on her website, alannamcfall.wordpress.com.

SHIPS PASSING IN THE NIGHT: ROMANCE & MARRIAGE BETWEEN LOVERS FROM ANTI-SYNCHRONOUS WORLDS

An essay by Specialist Estaugh Johnten,
as provided by Mickey Hunt

A frozen image of the park's playfield looks somewhat like an ordinary playfield on Earth. Families are sitting on blankets with their picnics, a canine is poised in the air as he clamps his teeth on a flying disk, a woman is jogging down the path between a row of shade trees. Children dash though a play castle with its hanging bridges and polymer towers. All this would look ordinary, except the colors in the image are antipodal like in an old-fashion film negative. What might be shadow emanates light, and it all incandesces with a lustrous glow.

An expectant crowd has gathered at the edge of a field, and upon closer inspection, you'd see that the postures and faces droop with sadness. They're faces possessing delicate contours no race of Earth ever had.

Even stranger would be watching the film in forward motion, because everything moves backwards: the people, the leaves on the trees, even the sounds of voices.

I myself am walking backwards, with my arm around the waist of a wife I've never met, and a charming child of mine with her arm wrapped around my neck. My wife is carrying my field notebook. I'm elated, and of course completely bewildered. As we walk in reverse toward the waiting crowd, I nearly stumble, because I can't see where we're going.

Children are playing a game nearby. One girl runs backwards

and stoops to leave a small white ball on the ground. As we pass, the ball springs up of its own accord and smacks me in the nose. It hurts ...

Welcome to the planet Lumen.

The above scenario describes my personal first minutes after I stepped to the ground of a planet circling the first dark star[1] we've ever discovered and located within a vast region of dark matter. It's a planet, indeed a whole region of space, where physics on its most rudimentary level, and, perhaps even time itself, moves opposite to ours.

Earth Command had engaged me on this exploratory mission for the remote possibility of encountering sentient beings on other worlds. While I have studied astrophysics as a hobby, my true expertise was in anthropology. My job was to catalog and analyze sentient alien cultural practices. Little did anyone guess that I would arrive on this new planet already "knowing" a great deal about life there. It was a knowledge that sprang into existence as events occurred. Of all our team members on the mission, I was the only one who could fully wrap his brain around how things worked. My Earth-based supervisors believe it was my Asperger's Syndrome that enabled me to adapt to the confusing environment. What had isolated me from other people in normal time allowed me to better fit in on Lumen. Plus, I had already developed attitudes and techniques to help me compensate for my misperceptions.

~

When our research ship *Radiant* first approached Lumen, we entered a high slow orbit above the nightside. The view from my port window showed the surface to be dark, that is, with no lights to indicate any sort of advanced civilization. I wrote in my field notebook, *Another lonely silent sphere, like me.* Only when the ship orbited to the dayside of the planet did our scouting telescopes show living beings with a technology similar to 20th century Earth; that is, they had self-propelled transport craft, including flying vessels. As I gazed from the window, a weird cluster of rocks about a kilometer or so from us flew away from the planet. I didn't learn until later that they were meteors falling *toward* the planet.

During Landing Orientation, I arrived late and took the remaining empty seat in the front row. Captain Therreal[2] remarked that it was strange the inhabitants hadn't responded to our attempts to contact them by radio.

At that time, Communications Officer Esang interrupted to shrilly announce that Lumen was being *bombarded* by messages from space, including one from a woman who cried in inverted English, "Please come back, we need you!" This was all a mystery that we resolved only later.

As we landed the transport shuttle on the surface for the first time ever, Assistant Safety Officer Sanderson was in charge of making one last check to the atmosphere's compatibility with human physiology. The composition of Lumen's air was roughly identical to Earth's, except in the motion of the elements' atoms. Sanderson reported the air was "okay," and as we waited for the transport's integument door to open, she noticed that I was clutching my notebook to my chest.

"Eager today, Professor?" she asked.

Suddenly self-aware and chagrined about looking like a schoolgirl, I nonchalantly lowered the notebook to my side. No matter how many times I corrected her, she always called me professor.

"I'm just messing with you," she said.

Oh. I realized then she was only teasing, but her use of "mess" reminded me of an archaic meaning of the term, that of a sailing ship's dining hall. This seemed like a natural segue, so I asked her if she would join me for dinner sometime.

She only grimaced and shook her head.

I suppose the universe wreaked its revenge when the door opened and flooded the compartment with the native air. Sanderson hyperventilated and passed out cold. The door buzzed and slammed shut, and medics evacuated her to a berth in the shuttle where she soon recovered. As it turned out, Sanderson never could process Lumen's air, and further research showed that approximately 5.5% of the *Radiant*'s crew couldn't. For them, the oxygen was totally inert and unreactive, and they were compelled to wear breathing apparatus and tanks whenever they spent time on the planet, a situation which was a burden. Also, as it turned out, Sanderson grew to respect me, and we became friends. She was a medical doctor, and I invited her to attend the birth of my daughter, a story I will return to later.

When the landing team shuffled down the ramp, I among them,

the scene before us appeared as a blazing impressionistic painting of a New England landscape. Figures approached from the crowd. They appeared blurry until they drew near, and I realized with a shock that they were walking in reverse. A person turned to me, and now I saw it was a young woman. She held a baby on her hip, a little girl almost a year old grasping her mother's blouse. The young mother's luminescent skin, garments, and facial features gave her a beauty I never imagined possible.

Her baby. She reminded me of photographs of my own mother when she was a child.

The woman stepped toward me and kissed me lingeringly on the mouth—her lips cool to the touch—and when she stepped back she held a garland of flowers in her free hand. A memory burst into existence, a memory telling me the sweet smelling lei had hung around my neck only seconds before. How was this happening? She spoke to me in a familiar, bizarre, inverted language.

As other crewmembers were greeted with similar, albeit less intimate farewells from the indigenous people, I felt myself swept up in astonished awareness that we and they existed within the same reality and were passing in converse directions—my future being the young woman's past, and my past being her future.

So that's when I realized the mysterious radio message had been for me, and the immense throng of people at the landing site had gathered to say goodbye.

My first impulse was to sprint back to the transport and hide in a locker, but for once in my awkward life, when everything was infinitely awkward, I knew what to do. I held my ground and began writing on my field notebook. The young woman lifted the garland to her nose and breathed in. She smiled like gentle sunlight, wiped her eyes, sniffed twice, and nodded with comprehension as droplets leapt from the ground, rolled up her cheeks, and squeezed into her tear ducts.

I finished writing and held up the notebook so she could read my words, *I love you and our baby very, very much. I promise, we will be together again.*

I swapped my notebook for our child who snuggled her face against my chest. And I had no idea how it all would work, but clearly we had already solved certain future problems of cross-cultural interaction—I had a family!

~

Is time real, or was it simply that the physics of Lumen moved backward, even at the quantum level? Is it that subatomic particles like electrons were just spinning in reverse to ours?

Up until we encountered Lumen, what we found there and in the planet's spatial neighborhood would have been described as being composed of Diroc's Antimatter.[3] However, the only antimatter we've known before has been in laboratories. We've never experienced antienergy before, not what was recognized as such. In artificial, simplistic experiments, whenever matter and antimatter touched each another, they annihilated. But the stable presence within our galaxy of antispace and all it contains, and our safe interaction with Lumen, proves that matter and natural antimatter coexist, which brought up the possibility that our previous theories have been all wrong.

Dr. Pachero-Nanez, the first scientist to clarify and popularize the idea that time was not real, said it's only a human construct that measures relative rates of change. Pachero-Nanez helped us understand that Einstein's theory of relativity wasn't as profound as once thought because it only meant that time seems to flow differently because of an observer's relationship to the light by which we perceive events. Our experience on Lumen proved Pachero-Nanez wrong.[4]

Why? Because my life with Ahtebazille existed *before* it had even happened from my perspective, we learned that time itself was a singular entity of its own. Time *is* real. And yet what happened was completely dependent on our decisions in that moving present that we shared together, a present something like the juncture of two streams when they form a river. The streams merge, mixing and churning, and continue on with both changed.

Events occurring in that present changed my past and created their own memories. As I already wrote, when Ahtebazille greeted me, she hung a lei around my neck as a parting gift. Until she took that action, it never happened for me, but when it happened, that lei continued to be around my neck in her future and in my past, and that's why I remembered it.

My two and a half years on Lumen was full of such experiences, but the confusion and continuous reshaping of my memory was only part of the difficulty.

~

Most people of Lumen were sad when we arrived, and sadness often pervaded my mood as well, because I knew I had such a brief period ahead to be a father and a husband. Our daughter Atte'eerneh was growing younger each day, and in a few months her contraction of size and abilities alarmed and grieved me. I knew what the inevitable would be. It was exactly like having a child with a terminal illness, but there was no treatment, cure, or hope of recovery. Her birth then was like a death, or at least a vanishing. I saw her slip into her mother's body, and then observed as Ahtebazille's belly shrank month by month, and I couldn't forget our daughter as she had been, happy, scampering around our house (backwards of course), playing with dolls and singing nonsense songs. I was so sorrowful in thinking that I couldn't know her at a period later in her life. Adding to the sorrow, when I arrived on Lumen, Ahtebazille was pregnant with our second child, a boy.

I had to force myself to not think about this.

~

For an example of a milder difficulty, as it turned out, arriving late to social events was essential on Lumen. In fact, to be early you had to arrive after an occasion was completely over, or you would be too late. By the time of Ahtebazille's and my wedding I had it figured out. Because, of course, from my point of view, the wedding ceremony began at the end and worked backwards to the beginning. In fact, our last ever "connubial celebration" took place on the night *before* the wedding.

Whenever I speak at holo-seminars and conferences, the most frequently asked questions are about sex. Everyone wants to know how to "make a baby" on Lumen. I've written about it in impersonal clinical detail in my paper "From Coitus to Foreplay: Sexual Relations Between Intraspecies Partners of Reverse Time Ecosystems,"[5] but it's enough to say in this present article that the process is far easier than one might imagine. As I have understood from the wide study of cultures, intimate relations between the opposite sexes are fraught with awkwardness, blunders,

18

embarrassment, misunderstandings, and even humor, obstacles often easily overcome in a loving relationship. When the respective time streams of the partners are opposed, those factors are compounded. But as with everything on Lumen, I was always surprised how well it worked out when we just relaxed and let what might happen, happen.

~

The same as with our daughter undeveloping until the point of when her life began at fertilization, so my relationship with my wife Ahtebazille diminished over time. I knew her better, but she knew me less. She seemed to have forgotten my favorite foods. Her cooking deteriorated. After the year and more of enjoying our marriage bed, the strictly enforced chastity was a sore trial for me. Her parents stopped liking me, saying that a close relationship between their daughter and me was impossible. She comprehended what I said less.[6] Beyond when we first met one evening at a square dance, I was a stranger to her, but I knew her better than ever, the situation being a mirror to when I arrived and first saw her. So, as we knew it would, my wife didn't know me anymore. Think of it like severe Alzheimer's, except she was young and healthy in every way, making the "memory loss" all the more painful.

~

Though we had been among the Lumens for a long while, they acted cold, cautious, and afraid, as if we had just arrived. When we actually had arrived, we were clumsy. Now they were, and you had to be on a continuous lookout for unexpected hazards, like being run over while crossing the street.[7] I myself was nearly killed by an ice cream truck roaring around a corner.

So, there was no longer any joy in staying, and after 30 full months of living on the planet, deeply involved in the affairs of its people, we lifted off for the last time, with me feeling even more alone than I have in my whole life.

~

That was eight months ago, and soon after my arrival on Earth

I ran into my old friend Mickey Hunt[8] at my favorite tea cafe. Mickey had been an obscure social reformer back in the 21st century and took up writing faux science fiction and fantasy in his retirement. I say faux, because the science and fantasy were really real. Captain Therreal had run across an actual copy of Mickey's early novel in a museum and went back to meet him. Therreal ended up inviting him on a time transcendence journey, but now after extensively roaming across Earth's eras, Mickey planned to return home to his own time. When he heard about my family on Lumen, and my heartbreak over how empty my current life was, he asked me to join him aboard the *Chariot* for the acceleration to light speed, a voyage that would last a whole year. He said he'd make room for me in his quarters.

"Really, you'd take me along?" I said. "Only a select few go on these expeditions."

"You'll be my guest," he said. "Here's what you do: when we break the light barrier, we leave the material-energy-chronos universe and enter what's called eternity. You know, 'God is light.' It's like dying, except you're not dead. It's being totally awake. In the dream world, your powers of thought and action are limited. Your mind floats along, flitting here and there, and you have negligible control over imaginary actions within the dream. Your body is all but immobile and paralyzed in bed. Consider that the supernatural world is to the natural world what the waking world is to the dream world. In the supernatural, you have incomparably more freedom and control over your mind and body than you do in your ordinary existence. You can go anywhere and anywhen you like." He paused to let this sink in, and then repeated, "Anywhere and when. It's the only way to travel anymore. Time and space transcendence."

A warm flush suffused my whole being, and the gloomy cloud that enveloped my head vanished entirely. I pulled out my field notebook and began scribbling my packing list.

Mickey said, "Why don't you tell me what you're thinking?"

I told him what, and that's my plan for the future.

Calculating my life expectancy, I intend to arrive back on Lumen so that I might possibly live until a few years before I arrived the first time. That will give me another 40-50 years with Ahtebazille and my children.

"Don't forget the grandchildren, great grandchildren, and so on," Mickey said. "You may be surprised at the multitude of descendants you have. I was when I peeked ahead, and knowing about them is why I never feel lonesome."

My enthusiasm suddenly fell away, and I closed my notebook. "I just thought of it. When I rejoin my wife, for her it will be parting all over again. She'll be old, maybe even dead."

"Can't be helped," Mickey said. "You've got to go."

He's right. And I will go.

~

[1] A dark star is a black hole in particular effects, but much lower in mass.

[2] This is the same Therreal who commanded the starship *UNS Chariot* in the first intentional time-transcendence excursions based on the theories of Nobel Prize winning propulsionist, Dr. Pachero-Nanez, who discovered that as a vessel neared the speed of light, its mass decreased, enabling it to break the light barrier and escape the limitations of the material-energy-chronos universe.

[3] Paul Adrien Maurice Dirac, 8 August 1902–20 October 1984.

[4] Pachero-Nanez was wrong in other things as well, namely his National Socialist politics.

[5] Originally published in the *Journal of Chaotic Terrain*, Vol. 3849, Issue 3, Year Indeterminate.

[6] I had taught her English and I, in turn, had to learn to speak and understand it backwards.

[7] I never quite learned to safely drive on Lumen.

[8] Not his real name.

———

Estaugh A. Johnten grew up on a farm in Pennsylvania and earned a B.A. in Social/Cultural Anthropology at Templetown University. He received a Fulhaus/DAD Fellowship for the Eberhard-Hostleter-Universität in Tübingen, Germany, where he subsequently completed a M.A. His work with the extraordinary voyage of the *UNS Radiant* was funded through a grant from the International Academies of Sciences, Medicine, and Engineering. When defending his Ph.D. dissertation at Hahvad University just prior to his departure from regular time, he told the examination committee to "Jump in the lake."

Mickey Hunt explores the universe from his base in Asheville, North Carolina. His reports disguised as fiction have appeared in the *Literary Hatchet*, *AntipodeanSF*, the *Dead Mule School of Southern Literature*, the *Dark Mountain* anthology, and elsewhere. Readers may learn more at chaoticterrainpress.blogspot.com.

A brief, flash-length version of this story originally appeared in *Penumbra*, November 2014, with a title of "Not the Wrong Planet."

A FICTIONAL SELL-OUT
An essay by L. Gordonsby-Wilkes,
as provided by Soren James

———————

Dedicated to people for whom the world has been tricked from them:

In Victorian England, it was common practice for an upper-class gentleman, when dressing for formal occasions, to enter a room with a low ceiling and to there perform a small jump, thus ensuring his hat was on properly. This practice began to die out in the 1880s due to a substantial number of neck injuries.

It was due to one of these neck injuries that a certain Lord "Dippy" Swanson was forced to give up rhinoceros hunting. Lord Swanson's frustration and ensuing boredom resulted in him attaining the job of minister for education to the British Empire. It was in this post that he had his most notable historical influence: altering the apparatus of the education system to include the red pen.

Having always found the blunders of youth repugnant, he was often anxious to highlight these mistakes. So in his new position in charge of the education system, he chose to underscore these errors in the most confrontational and aggressive colour available, believing that if the pen were to be truly mightier than the sword, then the pen, too, should be coated in blood.

A less historically observed fact about Lord Swanson was his surreptitious control of the means-of-production of red pens, which led to a gross disparity in working conditions. Almost single-handedly, he promoted the idea that red pen manufacture was a specialised process, requiring specialist workers. It was through these manipulations of perception that he managed to ensure lucrative business investments, and comfortable jobs, for many of his wealthy friends.

The increased disparity in working conditions that ensued saw factories that produced the more ubiquitous black pen having their already sub-standard working conditions decline further. Meanwhile, new and comfortable cottage-industries developed for the production of red pens.

This area of industry further amplified disparities in employment when Lord Swanson decreed that red pen production should employ only the highest graded (supposedly the most talented) students—generally those who had received more black pen-marks than red. While in contrast, the black pen continued to be mass produced in unhealthy conditions by "unskilled," and less valued workers—those receiving more red pen-marks at school.

Thus Lord Swanson had created an overarching system of control and division, wherein the rich were left producing red pens—and using them to summarily dismiss and subjugate the deprived with red crosses—while the poor grafted away producing black pens, providing the numerous ticks and encouraging comments that generally elevated the rich.

Somewhere along the way, Lord Swanson and his cronies had created a system that ensured the success of the successful (proving successful), while defeat remained constantly in the hands of the defeated. Thus a clearer and clearer differentiation between the two classes grew.

~

One day, I had the opportunity to approach Lord Swanson regarding these issues, but when I put the facts before him, he gruffly sought to dismiss me by saying, "Ridiculous! I have not been lining the pockets of wealthy friends, and clearly there is no difference in the manufacture of black or red pens. You're off your head, sir!" He then made to leave the gentleman's club, only to be prevented by two doormen who were sympathetic to my argument.

I proceeded to explain further to a trapped Lord Swanson that my father had worked in a black pen factory (labouring hard to pay for my education), and directly across the road from where we lived there existed a red pen industry. Every day we would see their wealth: the tailor-made hats, bespoke umbrellas, and all manner of custom accoutrements—items created by successful, "artisan" types.

This was in stark contrast to our side of the road, where we had mass-produced shoes, cloth caps, home-darned socks, and torn shreds. The products available to us were inferior, bulk-produced items, often stained with the sputum of sickly, slaving workers.

Moreover, I stated emphatically, on our side of the road people have been subjected to mechanised, assembly-line jobs, and alongside this, popularised mass-entertainments and intoxicating substances. Yet across the road, affluent people lived in their nourishing environments, with easy access to the arts and books, in an atmosphere conducive to the furtherance of learning.

Lord Swanson looked at me, his eyes quivering with indignant anger. I held his stare, expectant of an answer, our eye to eye stand-off lasting more than a minute.

Finally, Lord Swanson spoke. "Would you like to own a couple of those factories of which you are so jealous?"

"Yes." This concession fell shyly from my mouth.

"I can arrange that." He continued, his voice carrying the assurance of generations of advantage behind it. "There's only one condition: you pass all this nonsense off as a mere fiction."

L. Gordonsby-Wilkes (born Luke Gordon) was raised in the Northern English town of Rustingwart. His childhood was spent in dire poverty, of which he would later claim that the only toy he owned during these difficult years was piece of wood he'd named "Imposter."

As an adult, Gordonsby-Wilkes became a factory owner, eventually gaining a knighthood for his invention of the felt-tip pen. In 1901, he took over Felching Manor in the Surrey countryside, where he became increasingly reclusive until his suicide in 1914 (leaving a note that stated simply, "Imposter").

Soren James is a writer and visual artist who recreates himself on a daily basis from the materials at his disposal, continuing to do so in an upbeat manner until one day he will sumptuously throw his drained materials aside and resume stillness without asking why. More of his work can be seen here: http://sorenjames.moonfruit. com/writing/4585140878

DEMOTE THE EARTH
A Letter to the International Astronomical Union by
Professor E. Meritus, brought to our attention by
E. B. Fischadler

Sirs-

It has come to my attention that the IAU has been inconsistent and unfair in its treatment of Pluto. As is well known, Pluto has recently been demoted from the exalted status of "planet" to the lesser status of "minor planet." The IAU asserts that this demotion is in accord with established criteria for the designation of a planet: 1) The object orbits a star, 2) The object is roughly spherical, and 3) The object's gravitational field sweeps debris from its orbit.

Others have objected to the demotion of Pluto on various grounds. I do not intend to argue this point here. Rather, I wish to point out that the Earth also fails to meet the above mentioned criteria and so should also be demoted. Granted, Earth orbits the sun (despite the persistent belief by some that the universe is centered on them), and Earth is an oblate spheroid of low eccentricity, thus approximately spherical. An international society exists for the sole purpose of denying this,[1] but I shall go with the consensus here. It is the third criterion that Earth fails to meet.

While the earth may have swept debris from its orbit over several eons, this seems to have stopped sometime during the 1960s. In fact, Earth has gone so far as to join the other side, scattering junk throughout its orbit. Estimates of the number of such objects range into the thousands.[2] One has but to examine illustrations of Earth and its accompanying debris[3] to see this. These objects have been found to comprise primarily aluminum, titanium and silicon, all of which are found in significant quantities in Earth's crust.

According to the IAU, planets contribute to a tidy solar system by sweeping up junk in their orbits. Earth, on the other hand, is a litterbug. Many examples of debris originating on Earth and cluttering up the solar system are known to exist. Scientists have assigned names to these chunks of detritus, names like Telstar, ISS, and Shuttle. The last is particularly vexing. Each time a Shuttle re-enters the Earth's atmosphere, another is cast off within the year.

As if it wasn't enough that Earth litters its own neighborhood, several of these objects have been observed travelling to Earth's moon and beyond to other planets. These include Apollo, Viking, and Mariner. One such object has recently flown past Pluto (so now Earth is contributing to the debris that caused Pluto to lose its status as a planet. Ironic, isn't it?), and two such objects named Voyager I and Voyager II have travelled even farther, having left the solar system to pollute other star systems.

It is noteworthy that scientists have recognized and even exploited the fact that Pluto's largest moon Charon sweeps debris out of its orbit, providing a safe passage for the object designated New Horizons[4] on its way to polluting the far reaches of space. If Charon sweeps so clean and is not a planet, how can Earth, practically spewing space junk, be designated a planet?

Despite a rash of objections both in the scientific and popular press, the IAU refuses to budge from its designation of Pluto as a minor planet. I shall not endeavor to sway the IAU on this matter. Instead, I insist that in all fairness, the IAU must also demote Earth to minor planet status.

Professor E. Meritus

[1] http://www.theflatearthsociety.org/cms/
[2] http://www.thespacereview.com/article/1598/1
[3] http://stuffin.space/
[4] "Almost Time for Pluto's Close Up" K Chang, *NY Times* July 6, 2015

Professor E. Meritus holds a barber chair in Syncretism at the

Melinoe Institute of Technobabble. His publications include *Pluto: It's a Small World After All* and the seminal work *Original Publications on Recycled Paper—How Can That Be?*

━━━━━━━

E. B. Fischadler has been writing short stories for several years, and has recently begun publishing. His stories have appeared in *Mad Scientist Journal, Bewildering Stories, eFiction,* and *Beyond Science Fiction.* In addition to fiction, Fischadler has published over 30 papers in refereed scientific journals, as well as a chapter of a textbook on satellite engineering. When he is not writing, he pursues a career in engineering and serves his community as an EMT. Fischadler continues to write short stories and is working on a novel about a naval surgeon. You can learn more about Fischadler and access his other publications at: https://ebfischadler.wordpress.com/

YOUR STAR

A notice from the Ad Hoc Committee for Stellar
Distribution, as provided by Daniel Hudon

———

Somewhere in the Galaxy, our galaxy, the Milky Way, your star shines. It was assigned to you when you were born, and its light has been traveling the vast spans of interstellar space since long before then. From the time when Babylonian priests looked up from their ziggurats more than three thousand years ago, astronomers have been compiling star catalogues, and at their general assembly, held every three years, they parcel out the stars to all new members of humanity like confetti, making sure that everyone gets one.

Many people live their whole lives without ever knowing they have their own star. These are the same people who don't know that they have their own tree (somewhere on the Earth) or their own species of beetle (even if they have to share).

Because astronomers have much other business to attend to at their meeting, like understanding the nature of dark matter, or the latest evidence for dark energy, which is slowly tearing the universe apart, the announcement of the delegation of stars is scheduled simultaneously with other sessions where important research breakthroughs are sure to be announced. In 2006, it was bumped off the agenda entirely to allow more time for the debate that ultimately led to the demotion of the planet Pluto.

Consequently, those who find out they have their own star often discover the news by accident. They stumble across an announcement on the Internet, see an ad in the Classified section of the newspaper, or receive an anonymous email on their twenty-fifth birthday with a text that reads only: "Have you found your star yet?"

These announcements are a legacy of Henrietta Hertzsprung, who, from the 1930s to the 1970s, was the chair (and often the only member) of the Ad Hoc Committee for Stellar Distribution. Based at the University of Vienna, Professor Hertzsprung, daughter of the great stellar astronomer Ejnar Hertzsprung, compiled birth records submitted to her from hospitals around the world and assigned as many as one hundred thousand stars per day. No one knew exactly how she did it, but every few months, she requested another filing cabinet from the university to keep her voluminous files in order.

When Professor Hertzsprung took the podium at her last General Assembly in 1976, she brought with her a sheaf of paper as thick as a telephone book and, as was her custom, for fifteen minutes she read out an abbreviated list of names of people who were assigned stars since the previous meeting. Members of the audience applauded heartily.

But this time, Professor Hertzsprung continued with a short speech about the delegation of stars. She acknowledged the vanguard of young astronomers who argued that the practice had become "arcane, almost astrological," and proceeded to describe its noble history. As custodians of the universe, she said, astronomers had a duty to share their heritage in order to inspire and awe the masses. Over the previous two centuries, the delegation of stars had given political and cultural events a cosmic commemoration. In 1867, all the citizens of the newly independent country Canada were assigned stars in the constellation of Ursa Major, and in 1885, in honor of the 200th anniversary of the birth of Johann Sebastian Bach, all the townspeople of Bach's birthplace, Eisenach, Germany, were granted stars in the constellation Lyra, the only musical constellation.

The practice was not without its rewards, she said. Several biographers of Edgar Allan Poe indicated that he found his star just before penning the wide-ranging (and often prescient) speculations in his cosmological meditation, "Eureka," published as his last great work a year before he died in 1849. A century later, in 1953, a few writers speculated that Sir Edmund Hillary conquered Everest in the hopes of getting a better look at his star (it was cloudy). Some have said that the madness of the great telescope maker, George Ellery Hale, who built four of the world's largest telescopes, was provoked by the frustration of never finding his star. The famous lecture by "the learned astronomer" that Walt Whitman attended? It was about finding your star.

Because the stars belonged to everyone, Professor Hertzsprung vowed that the delegation of stars would continue after her retirement. She urged her fellow astronomers to stay abreast of the committee's notices and to remember their role as ambassadors for the heavens.

For some people, it is enough to know that they have their own star, and like a pleasant dream, the news makes them smile. Others begin a quest of finding their star, which, for city dwellers, due to the ubiquitous lights and frequent clouds, can take some time, perhaps years. So they manipulate their lives by taking extra business trips, planning vacations to far-off locations, or simply going for late-night weekend walks in the hopes of finding their star. If asked, they couldn't tell you why they are looking, except to say that it seems the right thing to do, like a gesture that's to be reciprocated. Or they will shrug as if it's a private duty for the fulfillment of some mysterious universal law.

A few people who openly admit to their quest have been known to suffer the petty criticisms of family and friends who hint that the task is akin to looking for the pot of gold at the end of the rainbow. Some soon give up. Some adopt an attitude of solemn seriousness, like those taking the pilgrimage to Santiago de Compostela in Spain or the circumambulation around Mount Kailash in Tibet. Like pilgrims everywhere, they trust in the sanctity of their journey and have faith that its ultimate meaning will become clear to them. Others have been known to knock on the doors of observatories in the middle of the night, begging for assistance in finding their star.

A thirty-five-year-old woman in Cuzco, Peru, recently got lucky and found her star, in the constellation of Cassiopeia, the first time she looked. She quit her job, left her lazy boyfriend, and moved to Buenos Aires to study Argentine tango. A fifty-two-year-old man in Istanbul, Turkey, found his star after searching for three years and reported that he'd never been happier in his life. A teenaged boy in Wales vowed to find his star by his twentieth birthday. He is now forty-seven years old and still looking.

Despite these stories, finding your star won't make you rich or lovable. It won't save your job or marriage. It will simply entice you into the mysteries of the universe and that alone makes it worth looking for.

When some people find out they have their own star, they try to find out everything they can about it. Usually, they want to know its size—whether it's larger than the sun, and how far away it is. Lately, they have been wondering if their star has its own planets. They also want to know if there's something special about their star. Invariably, there is, because no two stars are the same. Early in the 20th century, Annie Jump Cannon categorized and catalogued more than 200,000 stars for Harvard College Observatory in Cambridge, Massachusetts. She described each as an indisputable fact in a larger whole.

But sometimes the astronomers don't know all the facts, including, perhaps, the exact coordinates of your star. With larger telescopes that peer deeper into the Galaxy, and into the universe, astronomers are continually updating their catalogues. Because the stars are assigned in batches, many don't yet have actual catalogue numbers, nevermind known coordinates.

Make no mistake, your star wants nothing of you. It doesn't even care if you look for it. It's just there, a distant light in the night. You can make of it what you wish—a beacon in the dark, a channel for your thoughts, a work of art shining somewhere in the galaxy. It is a star, in hydrostatic equilibrium, its gravity finely balanced by the pressure of high temperature fusion reactions occurring millions of times each second. If the balance is lost, the star will shrink or expand, and its days will be numbered. Even so, for small stars, the end can be drawn out, taking not millions but billions of years. So, to be honest, the star has nothing to do with you and will outlast you. If it is a massive star, it will spend its life cooking up heavy elements and then spill them out into space, where one day a new solar system could form.

"How will I know it's mine?" you ask.

"It's shining just for you," the astronomers say, with a wink. "Only you can truly see it."

This answer may be unsatisfactory, and so some astronomers have been known to quote Professor Hertzsprung and give an encouraging nudge: "You'll know it when you see it."

It's true. Go outside tonight, crane your neck, and look in perfect silence at the stars. Your star is out there, somewhere, shining.

———————

The Ad Hoc Committee for Stellar Distribution meets irregularly but frequently in order to keep up with the increasing number of Earthlings. Because Earth's birth rate far exceeds the stellar birth rate, Committee members are presently discussing how to handle running out of stars to assign to new Earthlings. In addition, a large project of the Committee is to put its formidable catalogues in the Cloud with the idea of encouraging people to help others find their star. Although no Committee members have found their star, we are assured all are looking.

———————

Daniel Hudon is a product of the Big Bang, stardust, and evolutionary biology, in that order. He's a pessimist on intelligent life elsewhere in the universe, and an optimist for finding intelligent life on Earth. He is going to keep writing prose and poetry, and posting links to danielhudon.com, at least until he finds his star. Then he's going to retire and watch soccer full time.

AN ATHEIST'S GUIDE TO THE AFTERLIFE
An essay by Dr Quintum Magnamaby,
as provided by J. R. Hampton

For this report, I have implicitly assumed that there is an afterlife. This may not be so. There are three possibilities:

1. There is an afterlife.
2. The afterlife exists as a hypothesis based on infinite impossibilities, which can be regularly tested and proven by repeated lack of evidence.
3. There is no afterlife. The arbitrary observations are evidence of a deluded mind, and anyone encountering such should immediately seek medical attention at once.

In this account, I will share my observations on my own personal experience of the underworld and describe for the atheist the correct protocol, should they unexpectedly find themselves there.

I clambered and skidded down the path, too afraid to know or care what I was doing, and before I knew it, I found myself standing just a few feet from a large beast. It regarded me with little interest, having plenty already to chew on. A length of dripping intestine was hanging from its gnashing jaws, and its face was glistening with blood. Its pink gums displayed a rack of stained teeth, and its rancid breath, together with the hot fetid air of the chasm, combined into a stench so overpowering that my eyes were streaming, and I was overcome with nausea. I reached into my pocket and slowly took out my camera. Testing the angle, I pressed the button. Click, a selfie with the great mythological beast, Cerberus.

1. Check the Expiry Date

In which we learn how to respond appropriately to the dead.

It was now almost impossible to comprehend that only hours before, I'd been sat in the living room of a student's house, invited by someone I vaguely knew, attending what could only be described as an unsuccessful attempt at a New Year's Eve party.

The New Year had arrived as unceremoniously as I had departed. Unable to catch a taxi and unwilling to accept a lift from a bearded economics student, I took a shortcut through the woods.

The entrance to the underworld is as unspectacular as it is frustrating. I don't know whether it was the three shots of jellified vomit, out of date cocktail sausages, and soggy pretzels that I had consumed previously, or the overwhelming cordiality thrust upon me by a man who insisted that I called him Leo, which made me agree to go. I followed him through a small burrow and stumbled down a stone spiral staircase, which cautiously reminded you to "Mind your head" when the surface was uneven and "Uneven floor" after a brick had hit your head.

Leo guided me into a room that resembled the cellar of an abandoned 1960s hospital and disappeared through a door. The white painted walls were snaked with copper pipes that seemed to carry the hissing and gurgling of a distant un-serviced boiler. After a few uneventful minutes, a man dressed in blue overalls looked in on me, decided that he didn't like the look of me, and then disappeared back behind the door.

Moments later, he returned. He stood a few short feet away from me, wearing a face that resembled one that had just discovered that his reserved seat on a train had been occupied by an idiot. I pulled out my book and tried to hide in its pages. He asked me if I had a ticket; I said I hadn't. He then disappeared back through the door again.

After another few uneventful minutes, Leo returned and informed me that I was in the wrong place and led me through a corridor to another small white walled room. He asked me if I had a ticket, I said I hadn't, and he left the room.

Just as I was starting to get into my book, I was rudely interrupted by a man dressed like a bus conductor ought to. He asked me if I had a ticket; I said I hadn't. Shaking his head, he told me that I was in the wrong room and led me back to the room from which I'd previously been sent from.

My reading was once again rudely interrupted by a commotion from the corridor. Leo burst into the room, followed by the other two gentlemen. Leo asked me if I had a ticket; I said I hadn't. He grabbed my book from out of my hands, removed the bookmark, and passed it over to the bus conductor. The conductor clipped my bookmark and returned it to Leo.

An atheist should recognise that many people are not aware of an atheist in the afterlife. Therefore, such an atheist does not exist. These beliefs are strongly held as they help people to cope with their innermost basic neurosis. To respond appropriately with the dead, it is advised that the atheist keeps an open mind to what is not apparent to as much as what is ... such as an expiry date.

As we were ushered down a second corridor, Leo explained to me that I had made the men very upset, and we should try to move as quickly as possible. He also explained to me that my bookmark was the ticket and that I'd inherited it when I had borrowed this particular version of *The Divine Comedy*. He also explained to me that it was a promotional offer from Dante's Tours, the leading tour operators in the underworld.

I explained to him that it would have been a lot less troublesome if he'd explained all of this to me earlier.

~

2. Don't Lose Sight of the True Meaning of Death

In which we explore the commercial exploitation of being dead.

"Abandon all hope, ye who enter here."

The gates to Hell are something altogether much more interesting. It was here that I first met Dante. In appearance, he was the complete opposite of what you would expect a 14th century Florentine poet to look like.

He paced anxiously to and fro under the gateway. His eyes lit up as they caught sight of Leo and me approaching, and then pushing his way past the crowds, he quickly informed me of the arrangements.

"You're late! You've cocked everything up!"

He told me that because I was late, we'd have to wait for the next ferry, so I took the opportunity to take a look around. The porch to the underworld reminds one very much of a gothic cathedral. Ivy clings on to the old stone and spreads along the ancient crumbled walls in which occasionally a gargoyle will peep. One gets the impression that in the absence of the countless merchandise stalls, customary beggars, and piped recordings of howls and wailing, previous generations would have trembled in their boots at the sheer malevolence of the place.

Of course, it is not only the atheist who has difficulty with the idea of an afterlife. In 1985, upon witnessing the underworld, the American televangelist, the Very Reverend Reginald Dwight-Webb, immediately renounced his belief and converted on the spot to disbelief. He now runs one of the most successful apostasy services in the afterlife, helping thousands of souls find a new conviction of uncertainty, all, of course, at an ever increasing profit.

Dante directed me down an embankment through the crowds. After displaying his pass to a centaur, who insisted on checking it twice, we clambered on-board the ferry. The boat was crammed with a recently deceased group of Japanese tourists. Dante left me at the port window as he rushed off to find out why we hadn't been upgraded.

As we made our way across the Acheron River, a flurry of cameras began to excitedly flash. With my sleeve, I wiped away the condensation, and squinting, saw through the mist an old man gripping onto the sides of a small wooden boat. The waves of our ferry rocked him violently on the river's choppy surface, and his long white beard fluttered in the wind as he desperately tried to recover his oar.

"That's Charon," Dante informed me as he returned with two hot coffees in polystyrene cups. "For hundreds of years, he used to ferry the deceased across this river."

I watched with incredulity as Charon attempted to steady himself before a final wave knocked him off his feet, which duly followed the rest of him overboard in one great splosh.

"He still insists on doing it, even though everyone takes this ferry nowadays," Dante continued. "Says he was here first. Stubborn old fool."

~

3. We Don't Talk About It

In which we recognise people's rights not to be recognised.

A short walk after disembarking from the boat, we came to the edge of a precipice. Looking down, the land is twisted and fractured on such an immense scale that your mind is completely at a loss on how to process it. Jagged mountain peaks and fiery clouds stir above vast rivers of ice, which crack inch by inch through unfathomable ravines.

For many centuries, the exact geographical composition of the underworld has been hotly debated. However, a simple trick can be applied. If one is to hold out a pencil at arm's length in any direction, and close their left eye, then one will see the actual curvature of the pencil against the background. Many atheists use this fact as incontrovertible proof that the afterlife is the creation of a warped mind.

I followed Dante along a gritty path to a station. Obediently, I stood in line behind him.

"We have to take the cable car down to the First Circle of Hell," he explained. "It is here that we will see Limbo—the place reserved for the virtuous heathen."

As we descended, I took in the view. Only metres away from the cable car, huge cataracts thundered and roared down into the narrow valleys below. I watched with unease as a small child clung onto its mother's hand whilst the car shuddered and trembled under the rickety cables. It occurred to me then that this was the first time I'd truly felt scared since descending into hell.

By all accounts, Limbo is a rather pleasant place. A field stretches out in all directions, surrounding a castle ruins. Trampling our way through the tall grass and thistles, Dante took to a bit of celebrity spotting. Enthusiastically, he pointed out a plethora of historical figures. Here was Socrates, there was Plato. Ptolemy, Euclid, Orpheus, Hippocrates, and Democritus, he boasted. I have to confess, I could not distinguish one toga clad oddball from another.

Whilst we, or rather I should say I, was puffing and panting up a small hill, we encountered a dear friend of Dante's.

After a brief introduction, Dante explained to me how it was Virgil who first suggested the idea of a tour company. Checking his watch, Dante told me that I could take a few minutes to have a wander as he and Virgil had some important paperwork to attend to. They disappeared together into a portacabin, so I headed toward the ruins.

Whilst I was perched upon a mossy stone watching the cable cars moving up and down the cliffs, I was approached by a tall and quite friendly gentleman who was handing out leaflets. He explained to me that he was a member of the Atheists' Camping and Caravanning Club and asked me if I believed in God. I said I didn't, so he handed me a leaflet.

The leaflet included, amongst other things, a five step plan on how to deal with the afterlife and a helpline for those who just couldn't get their head around the whole dying and waking up again thing.

It is important to note that for the atheist that resides in Limbo, there are some topics that are considered socially taboo. Although the situation appears to present evidence of a theist's point of view, an atheist's existence in the afterlife is still to be scientifically proven. Therefore, an atheist will not acknowledge their or anybody else's existence without firm empirical data. It is not up to the atheist to disprove the existence of an afterlife, but on the theist to provide a rationale for what the hell is going on.

From out of the smoky haze of a nearby barbeque, I saw Dante beckoning me down. In my haste, I stumbled right into the path of an elderly gentleman, passing right through him.

I turned to apologise and was met by an inquisitive wriggle of his moustache. It wasn't until sometime later that it dawned on me just who that man was. It was none other than Albert Einstein himself.

~

4. The Seven Hundred Year Itch

In which we learn that when something gets stuck in one's mind, it's hard to get it back out.

The Second Circle of Hell is reserved for the carnal sinners. We'd made our way down a sodden gulley and sheltered under a corrugated roof to escape the lashing winds.

Dante was negotiating for a discount at the booth and was becoming increasingly agitated. Exasperated he turned to me. "Bloody bureaucracy!" he raged.

He went on to describe that this was the true beginning of Hell, and the miserable git attending the booth was King Minos. Minos had once enjoyed his job as a judge in the underworld. For centuries, he'd assigned the fate of the damned by using his tail to show them in which circle of Hell they were to reside. This had brought him much joy, but now, under mounting legislature, mostly from the unceasing amount of lawyers descending into Hell, he was pinned down to his desk and was not in any mood to entertain us.

After a further few hours of negotiating, Dante managed to get us a pass into the Second Circle. Along the walk, Dante kept his eye on his watch, whilst I kept mine on the scenery.

The physics of the afterlife are very complex due to the fact that the majority of its residents are spectres. This causes a lot of frustration, particularly for physicists, and a great deal of embarrassment for everyone else. This can be summarised in Newton's fourth law of motion, published posthumously, which states that "for every interaction, there is an equal and opposite overreaction."

Below rows of red streetlights, parts of naked limbs illuminated from out of the darkness. Under the flickering neon lights of Cleopatra's Pleasure House, leather-booted women erotically danced behind glass windows. Gyrating men and latex clad centaurs jigged for multitudes of stirred souls beneath the doorway of Dido's Speakeasy. And masses of spirits clambered into one another for the thrills awaiting at the next phantom peep show.

Considering the obvious physical constraints of sex in the afterlife, one's insatiability for it actually intensifies when it becomes clear that it is no longer available.

It has been reported that some souls remain perpetually frustrated in this circle for their entire deaths; however, on average, it takes approximately seven hundred years for a soul to finally distract themselves with more spiritual pursuits, such as incorporeal crossword puzzles or spectral Sudoku. This is commonly referred to as the seven hundred year itch and is a cautionary tale to all living beings that engaging in more intellectually stimulating activities now can be of great benefit and relief in later years.

Whilst Dante considered which way to proceed, we temporarily stopped outside of Casanova's Nightclub, from which a poster advertised tonight's evocative show staring the beautiful Marilyn Monroe. Sensing my hesitation to continue, Dante ushered me through a darkened alley.

Somewhere through the passageway, I lost my guide and with hands stretched out before me, I slipped and skated along the sodden ground searching for something to steady myself on. I came to an opening. A hard driving rain made the path before me a treacherous one. To avoid the downpour of hail, I clambered and skidded down the path, moments later to be confronted with the great mythological beast known as Cerberus.

A sudden upwind alerted the beast to my presence. Its nostrils sniffed feverishly at the air. From its three heads, six devilish red eyes set themselves upon me, and a deep growl rumbled from its foul gut.

Gingerly, I let one foot after another trudge backward through the putrid sludge and silently edged my way out of sight. I ran aimlessly in any direction other than the one I'd been.

~

5. Thought for Food

In which we learn that it is all just a matter of taste.

The human mind can consume over a whopping 80 pounds of processed meat in under twelve minutes. The flavours of this feast are manufactured by an array of mental stimuli which include the colour, shape, texture, and brightness of the imaginable food. The biological process is irrelevant to the deceased.

This explains why there are so many restaurants throughout the afterlife. Many years ago, lamb and beef were very popular, and therefore many gods would insist that these animals should be offered as gifts so that they could gorge on their spectral goodness. Nowadays, the taste buds of the dead are a lot more sophisticated, and a top dead chef will have to search far and wide for the latest discarded tofu or chicken tikka masala. Contrary to popular belief, hamburgers are in fact very difficult to come by. This is because many of the fast foods we consume lack moisture and therefore refuse to decompose.

The menu at the bar and grill is considerable. The fat waiter stood over me impatiently before recommending the burgers. Who'd have thought that only minutes earlier, I'd been face to face with the front end of a 1960s British Leyland coach, and now I was being served burgers by none other than Elvis Presley himself!

The coach had recently been acquired by Dante's Tour Operators after it had hurtled fifty metres over a cliff in North Wales whilst crammed with sightseeing pensioners on a retro holidaying package.

Recognising the face I was wearing was not one that was enjoying itself, along with the discomfort my buttocks were experiencing from the coaches lack of suspension, Dante suggested that we visit Presley's Bar and Grill.

It was with a mouthful of French fries and a blob of ketchup on his chin that Dante explained to me, between bites, that we were now in the Third Circle of Hell. "This circle is for the gluttons," he spat.

~

6. Check the Small Print

In which we discover why bad things happen to good people and good things happen to bad people.

Back on the coach, we tumbled and bundled down the steep twisting roads and entered a valley of rocks that rose from the ground like enormous skyscrapers. The coach screeched to a halt at the foot of one rock where a casino had been erected.

Exiting the coach, Dante guided our eyes upward and, using a pair of rusty coin operated binoculars, I watched swarms of bankers ascending the rocks. They scoffed at great sacks of money at the top of the towering mountains. As they choked on the loot, some bankers would regurgitate coins. At the foot of the mountains, gamblers tore at each other for the fallen bounty to spend in the casino.

The odds of winning in the casino are very peculiar. Whilst observing a group of souls around a roulette wheel, I noticed that the ball fell in black 26 times in a row. The souls instantly began betting against black, assuming that a red streak was immediate. Moments later, they were again fighting one another for the sickly coins spilled along the ground.

"This is the Fourth Circle of Hell," Dante explained. "This is reserved for the hoarders and squanderers." After consulting his watch, he hurried us back onto the coach.

Before leaving this circle, we passed the financial quarter of Hell.

The Demonic Bank of Hell was founded in the 11th century by Pope Benedict IX. The bank offers the recently deceased an opportunity to pass on their sins to their descendants. For example, someone who has committed fraud in their lifetime can secure an exchange rate of poverty for a nominated descendant. This in turn will increase the descendant's chance of committing larceny, thus increasing the bank's soul assets.

If no direct descendant is viable, a spectre can select any living relation. Due to a limited range of ancestors, this clause allows one to freely select any living human being. This explains why bad things happen to good people.

This is known in the afterlife as Demonomics.

An alternative is available. Afterlife insurance, also known as Afterlife cover, is a way to help protect your loved ones spiritually after you have died.

It could be important if they have any broken promises, outstanding karma, or were in the midst of an extramarital affair upon your death. Afterlife insurance could help pay off these sins before they die, or it could help your family with everyday death costs. It could even help cover reincarnation expenses too.

A person can take out insurance for as many people as they like; however, exclusions may apply, such as the policy becomes null and void if the insured commits suicide.

An afterlife insurance company calculates the premiums to fund claims, costs, and profit. The cost of insurance is determined by the probability, likelihood, and opportunity of the occurrence by the insured for an event such as larceny, blasphemy, murder, or adultery.

Interest rates vary, and so it is advisable to check the small print before taking out a policy. Payments can be returned in many ways, such as being poked in the orifices with hot irons, being tied to a burning wheel, having one's innards eaten out by hungry birds, or being called insulting names. This explains why good things happen to bad people.

Of course, the modern atheist does not believe a word of this. Demonomists warn that if the modern atheist rate continues to rise, a crash in the Demonomy is unavoidable.

~

7. Don't Take it Personally

In which we learn that it's their problem, not ours.

The coach navigated its way through the valley for a few hundred metres, jolting down the narrow winding roads, before coming to a stop next to a jetty. Whether it was from the swishing purée of greasy burgers in my gut, the sweltering heat, or fusty stench of the swampy water, I accordingly threw up.

As we waited for the boat, I took a moment to make some sense of my surroundings. There must be some logical and rational explanation. Was the world I found myself in the result of some sort of mental breakdown, was this merely a very lucid dream, or was I essentially witnessing some kind of astral plane? It even occurred to me that I may have somehow accidentally entered into someone else's head.

Suddenly becoming aware of the disgusted looks aimed toward me from the other beings in the queue, I immediately stopped thinking.

Thinking out loud is considered extremely rude in the afterlife and highly unorthodox. It is preferable to keep such things inside of one's own head and completely unacceptable to impose it on others.

Dante hurried me onto a waiting boat. The rest of the passengers shot me rather irritated glances as the boat slightly sank under my weight.

The captain of the boat, Phlegyas, commenced with a commentary through a screeching microphone. I managed to ascertain that we were on the River Styx.

Although the afterlife is non-discriminatory toward believers and non-believers alike, many religious followers feel that they have exclusivity in the underworld. This is not the case. It is important for the atheist to assert their rights.

Belief is not a prerequisite for being dead and nor should it be. In fact, many of the longest inhabitants of the afterlife outdate even civilization itself and most certainly any concept of religion, and so found their passing no more bizarre than we'd find leaving a public toilet to arrive in Luton airport.

The motion of the boat was beginning to take its toll, and I found myself once or twice accidentally swaying into the middle bits of other passengers, to a condemnation of huffs and titters.

Precariously clutching my stomach, I huddled over the side of the boat to throw up into the foul Stygian marsh and was shocked to see an angry face scowling back at me through the musty water. Captain Phlegyas broken commentary explained that this was the Fifth Circle of Hell, and those condemned to spend eternity within the sludge of sanitary products, supermarket trolleys, faeces, and old boots, were the wrathful.

~

8. The City of Dis

In which we discover how to have one helluva good time!

Only those unfortunate enough to have been hit full on in the face by a lamp post could truly appreciate the effect that the great City of Dis has on one when seeing it for the first time.

The brochure describes how Dis is a perfect destination for families, couples, and groups. It is renowned for its exquisite architecture, cobbled streets, mausoleums, and wealth of visitor attractions.

The flaming sepulchres that surround the old town walls are one of its most popular sights, attracting over ten million tourists per day. With a one day pass, you can receive a 15% discount on selected attractions, including The Mausoleum of Pope Anastasius,

The Dis Dungeon, The Demonic History Museum, and an award winning evening ghost walk.

I eagerly placed a tick next to each attraction as I queued under the colossal gates of Dis. I dejectedly crossed out each attraction as it became obvious that we were not going to gain entrance to the great city any time soon.

The queue was becoming quickly agitated. The person behind me impatiently huffed, "You spend your whole life trying to avoid coming here and then when the opportunity arises, they make it so damned difficult in get in!" I had to agree. "What's the hold-up?" he tutted.

The hold-up, as it turns out, was me! Three hell-bent Furies that attended the turnstiles had noticed that I was not dead, and being "not dead" was something that they took particular exception to.

Dante, sensing trouble, motioned to me to step back as Tisiphone, flanked by Megaera and Alecto, launched into a furious tirade. Their hideous faces were smeared with copious amounts of eyeliner, lipstick, and blusher, flanked by locks of snakes.

The anatomy of the Furies is of great scientific interest. An amateur and little known scientist, Doctor Percivility, first proposed in 1880 that they were indeed an evolutionary offshoot from the pterodactyl. Upon discovering the skeletal remains of a Fury during an expedition to Crete, Dr Percivility presented his findings to the Royal Society. He was immediately branded a charlatan, and his specimen was debunked as a forgery. His protestations were dismissed, and the prevailing consensus by his peers was that Dr Percivility had mistakenly mixed up the remains of several bats, snakes and lizards, thus destroying his reputation for life.

In death however, he is regarded as one of the foremost leading experts in the anatomy of beasts. His paper on the evolution of mythological creatures is the underworld's highest selling science book of all eternity and well worth a read.

I studied with interest the crinkly semi-clad bodies of the Furies and their peculiar bat wings and claws.

"Fetch Medusa!" the Furies wailed. "Let's turn him to stone!"

As I stood with my eyes squeezed tight, Dante called in a favour. A Cherubim Officer had arrived on the scene, wagged his finger at the Furies, gave us a lecture on safety, and escorted us through the gates, where Dante agreed that we'd go straight to the hotel and stay out of trouble.

Ye Old Pandemonium Hotel is not a place one can sleep easily. The small, clammy room emanates an overwhelming odour, which gives the impression that a week old festering Doner Kebab lurks in some hidden corner. The bed frame struggles to hold a cumbersome mattress, the window is clearly distressed, and the kitsch 1970s orange décor invites you to add a splash of colour yourself. After depressing myself further by reading through the list of missed attractions that the brochure boasted, I decidedly left the hotel at once and began to explore.

Under neon lights, intoxicated centaurs staggered down Sixth Circle Street whilst demonic whores lay face down in pools of vomit. This was more like it!

In search of a cool drink, I found myself in a crowded bar. Soul upon soul swayed through me as I clutched onto my beer and looked for a quiet corner. A quiet corner was hard to find as thunderous music boomed from a little stage.

From my table, I gained a clear view of the ragged band, and oh what a band! The psychedelic twangs and riffs that whizzed around my skull were being shaped from the Stratocaster of none other than Jimi Hendrix! The crashing and rhythmic walloping beat of the skins were coming from Keith Moon's drumsticks, and the deep holler of Jim Morrison thundered through my whole being like a juggernaut.

Stupefied, I turned to the soul next to me to check that I was still, in fact, in Hell.

I was as shocked as the face staring back at me. The face was exactly the same face as the one that had belonged to my old history teacher from school, Mr Goodenough.

"What the hell are you doing here?" he yelled.

My brain was having a particularly hard time today, and by the expression on my face, Mr Goodenough could sense that my brain had now completely abandoned me. Over one or ten more drinks, he explained to me that his new found enthusiasm was no longer for history, but for the future.

He explained how time was a bit wiggly in the afterlife, and that the dead could see events from the future as clearly as those from the past. He warned me to avoid chicken nuggets, advised me against betting on the New Orleans Saints, reiterated the importance of brushing one's teeth, and finally, to always beware of a plastic Jesus.

The next thing I remember, my head was drumming in sync with "Purple Haze," and my hotel room wall was on its side. The orange décor startled me out of my stupor, and I accordingly threw up.

~

9. Don't Take it Too Seriously

In which we discover that death is too short to worry about trivial matters.

Dante was obviously upset about something. He waited until we were on the funicular descending to the Eighth Circle of Hell until he finally broke his silence.

"What was all that about?" he said in his stupid, condescending Florentine voice. "How would you like it if I spoke to you in the way you addressed the Minotaur?" he went on. "You totally embarrassed me back there."

I wasn't in the mood for grumpy demons and hot fiery sands today. Was it my fault that I needed to urinate? No one told me that those thorny trees were the souls of those who had committed suicide. How was I supposed to know that Hellhounds shouldn't be tickled behind their ears? Who wouldn't ask *that* question to a centaur? By the time we had reached the Malebolge, Dante had chirped up a bit.

The Malebolge, Dante explained, have recently undergone a regeneration project. The ditches—or Bolgia—each contain sinners for a specific punishment, and one can now safely walk upon them as they have recently been covered with Perspex glass. As we skidded above the Simonists, panderers, falsifiers, and astrologists, we took photographs whilst pulling silly faces, and soon our moods lifted. In one instance, Dante mimicked one of the sinners who was forced to carry around his severed head like a lantern. I almost died of laughter!

It quickly became apparent that the demons who patrol the Malebolge didn't share the same sense of humour as us, so we hastily made our way to the centre, where we would descend to the ninth and final circle of Hell.

The modern sceptic may have considerable trouble in believing the next passage, and so is advised to skip to the last passage of the story ... now.

~

10. Last Orders

In which we learn that we shouldn't waste our time.

Vexilla regis prodeunt inferni

When going to meet the Prince of Darkness, nothing beats arriving by helicopter with Wagner's "Ride of the Valkyries" blasting from a loudspeaker. I have to admit, Dante had really thought of everything. No wonder he was a poet!

The blades of the helicopter rotor spun mere inches from the towers of rock that encompassed us, before the pilot skilfully landed upon a sheet of frozen ice on the Cocytus River.

Dante and I fought against the icy gusts, and then, as if seeing a mighty mountain appear from out of a blizzard, I set my eyes upon Satan.

From three ugly faces, three revolting mouths gnawed upon the bodies of Adolf Hitler, Judas Iscariot, and Joseph Stalin. Their ripped and shredded torsos spilt down his chins like chewing tobacco. His body was buried waist deep in the ice. His black skin, cracked like old leather, wore gigantic withered wings.

An announcement rang from a Tannoy, "5 minutes 'til closing, would all visitors please make their way to the exits. Thank you."

As Dante and I approached the red rope barriers, I could taste the foul stench of Satan's breath. His sad eyes rolled down and made contact with mine. It occurred to me then that if anyone needed an Atheist's Guide to the Afterlife, it was him. I reached over the barriers and handed him the crumpled guide that I'd acquired in Limbo. Taking it between his weary fingers, he paused for a second, signed it, and then passed it back. It was then, in that moment, that I truly discovered what hell really was.

~

11. You're a Long Time Alive

In which we learn to make the best of what we have.

The human mind has a complex way of processing such an unimaginable sight ... it shuts down.

As I regained consciousness, Dante guided me to an elevator. "I hope you enjoyed the trip, Doctor."

I had.

The elevator had an unimaginable number of numbers, the topmost being Heaven and several numbers down, Purgatory. I asked Dante if I might visit these next, but he kindly pointed out to me, that as an atheist, there was nothing for me to see there. And so I returned to the surface of the Earth.

The elevator doors opened to a shower of bright sunlight. After the torment and savagery I had witnessed, this world felt surprisingly familiar. This world of fast-food restaurants, nightclubs, angry motorists, traffic wardens, and betting shops, this world, where bankers, beggars, corporate whores, and drunkards flood the pavements.

This world, of loans, mortgages, interest rates, and credit cards, of instant mash and celebrities, high speed fibre optic pornography, reality TV, gratuitous violence, corrupt politicians, and cheap commodities.

This world of dental plans, spy-cams, advertising slogans, and email scams, of fried chicken, secret societies, chewing gum, and nuclear bombs, of cocktail sausages, fur coats, pyramid schemes, cocaine, and anti-wrinkle cream.

To find my bearings, I searched for a sign. Stepping forward, I was instantly hit by an oncoming truck. The last thing I remember seeing was, steadily perched upon the dashboard, the face of a plastic Jesus looking back at me.

~

12. Conclusion

In which we ask ourselves whether the afterlife is worth pursing and speculate what comes next.

It is reasonable for a reasonable person to ask whether future examination into the afterlife is worthwhile. I would argue that further research would lead to very tangible benefits. It is hard to quantify these exact benefits without first experiencing some personal symptoms of death; however, if we were to invest in a rigorous scientific analysis now, it may result in a better world for the next generation.

As an atheist, I concede that this report may test the non-beliefs of others. It was written with the sole purpose of examining the mental, physical, and social implications of an afterlife and certainly has no intention of offending anyone's disbelief.

"An Atheist's Guide to the Afterlife" is available, should anyone require it, at the gates of the underworld.

Dr Magnamaby is a theoretical physicist at the London College of Hypothetical Science. His papers on the tangled cosmic helix, swirly black bits in space, and the social habits of muon neutrinos have been widely praised and published in peer-reviewed journals. The smallest object in the asteroid belt, Magnamaby B4C1, is named after him.

J. R. Hampton is a writer based in Coventry, United Kingdom. His stories have appeared at *Tethered by Letters*, *Flash Fiction Magazine*, *Hoot*, and *The Flash Fiction Press*. He writes sci-fi, humor, and mysteries.

A FORMAL APOLOGY FOR
RECENT DEVELOPMENTS

A letter by Hansel Calloway, as provided by Church Lieu

––––––––––

To Whom It May Concern:

It has come to my attention that my most recent paper, as published in the *Vanguard* journal on applied artificial intelligence, drew incomplete conclusions from my experimental data. I would like to offer my greatest, most sincere apologies for any harm that this may have caused to the scientific community. And, of course, to human civilization at large.

I understand that, since the results of my paper appeared to neatly resolve the facial-recognition and aggression errors present in numerous civilian droid models, it enjoyed a significant amount of publicity and praise. A reliable method to keep domestic and industrial robots from "going Frankenstein" on their owners was, understandably, a cause for relief. But the real turning point, or the "beginning of the end" for the dramatically minded, was when sensationalist web culture sank its claws into my findings. If I may be so bold, I recommend that you direct some of your blame towards websites and social media pages like "Science Is [Freaking] Cool." As is their *modus operandi*, they plastered wildly aggrandized versions of my *results* on Facebook walls and Twitter feeds while barely mentioning my *methods* or *experimental limitations*.

If they had taken more than a cursory glance at my research, they would have found that I designed the procedure for controlled, isolated use within closed—and I repeat, *closed*—robotic networks. To be fair, I may not have made this point quite clear enough. But I doubt that anything short of an all-capitalized declaration of "ONLY USE ON CLOSED NETWORKS" would have dissuaded them. In any case, I naively believed that I would have some time to refine and elaborate on my work before applying it in practice, assuming that my results would not be immediately pounced upon by the hyenas of sensationalism.

Unfortunately, my findings immediately caught the interest of robot manufacturers. When corporate eyes looked at my research, all they saw was a swift and definitive end to the lawsuits pouring in daily from angry customers. Software patches, littered with derivative code, popped up almost overnight.

I suppose I can't blame them that much. How could they, with their eyes fixed on the promise of financial security, have detected the oversight at the core of my work? So, when General Consumer Robotics released Patch Delta-1 into their *open*-structure network, the code collapsed catastrophically under the strain of supporting millions of robotic subsystems, instead amplifying the aggressive tendencies it was meant to curb.

I have developed a possible solution to the current predicament. But as you all are aware, we are greatly pressed for time due to the relentless advance of the homicidal metal hordes that were once our trusty vacuum cleaners, artificial surgeons, and hunter-killer drones. So rather than sitting through the lumbering, bloated bureaucracy of peer review, I have decided to take matters into my own hands.

As I write this letter from my underground bunker (defended by drones operating on a CLOSED network), I am putting the finishing touches on a virus to eradicate the corrupted code. I will infect the local robot population currently besieging my bunker with the virus, and pray that it disseminates through the general population.

God, I hope this works.

Sincerely,
Hansel Calloway, Ph.D.

––––––––––

Hansel Calloway, Ph.D., is a computational roboticist and the author of over two hundred papers in his field. He was required to step down from his position as Chair of the Department of

Robotics at the Tyrell Rosen University of Technology due to the "Crush, Kill, Destroy" scandal, but he managed to retain his position as a tenured professor.

—————

Church Lieu is a Los Angeles native and Cal State Los Angeles student currently working towards his bachelor's degree in Philosophy. He recently joined the staff of his school's literary magazine, *Statement*, and he is an aspiring speculative fiction writer with a love of all things robotic.

WRONG GUY

An essay by Jake "The Hammer" Hurley,
as provided by Michael Rettig

I sat in the back of the old wooden fishing boat, gripping the outboard motor handle with white knuckles. I'm a member of the most powerful gang in the country. My grandmother calls me a thug. But a thug that tonight was rising up in the ranks of my gang. I was nervous as hell in this stupid small boat in the dark heading to a small island in the middle of Mexico nowhere. My organization rose to the top by two things. Our ability to put hits on anyone and special weapons from the evil genius of Dr. Frombeck.

Frombeck was a German professor involved in poison gas research during the Great War. He'd left Germany after the defeat and now lived alone in a big house on a small tropical island off the coast of Mexico. He charged a hefty price for his inventions, but they were worth it. His pocket brain disruptors had helped us gain control over the Tongs in San Francisco. His tasteless poisons had let us wipe out the Marcesi brothers in Cleveland.

Two weeks ago, Frombeck had sent a coded message. He had a new brilliant discovery that would gain us more advantage.

I slowed the boat and pulled it into the small wooden dock on the island. The guy who usually came to pick up new inventions had been riddled with machine gun bullets by the Capone mob last month. I tied up the boat, then with the leather bag full of cash in hand, followed the instructions to walk up a jungle trail until reaching the two-story stone house. Banging a big brass knocker in the shape of an imperial German eagle on the massive front door, I straightened my double-breasted suit and the tilt of my fedora.

After a few minutes, bolts unlocked from inside.

The door swung open. Backlit was the man himself. Tall, cadaverous, wearing an immaculately starched, ankle-length white lab coat with a black leather belt and holster cinched at the waist. In one hand was an odd looking pistol, pointed at me.

"The password please."

"Long live the Kaiser!"

"Where is the man who came before?"

"He got killed. I'm the new guy."

"You have the money?"

I lifted up the bag.

"Good."

"I've got tell you, Herr Doctor, the boys back home are sure looking forward to your next invention."

"Pshaw, those previous ones were nothing but children's toys compared to what I have for you."

The old German gave off the scents of tropical mold, cigars, and rancid sauerkraut. I kept looking at the odd looking pistol.

"Come, my good man, let me show you what you will have for your money."

Leading me through dark hallways, Frombeck finally unlocked the last door with a key. He opened the door with a flourish and ushered me inside. The professor switched on the lights. It was a laboratory. A generator running was background noise while a record player played classical music. There were dozens of small cages on racks around the room. It smelled like a dirty reptile house at a zoo. I sneezed. What a stink.

"*Gott Im Himmel!*"

Frombeck drew his odd looking pistol and shot dead a rat the light had sent scrabbling in the corner. I stared at the pistol. It had been virtually silent. Reaching down to pick up the ejected casing, I saw it was a standard .45 caliber cartridge. I smiled at the advantage my gang would have.

"Sir, this is brilliant. Well worth the money."

Frombeck saw me staring at the pistol.

"No, no, this is just a toy. You are not buying this, you simpleton. This is what you are buying."

He waved at the cages. I walked closer and peered inside the cages. In each was a little box turtle with two copper wires stuck in its head. All the wires led to a large wooden box with a typewriter keyboard.

"I have discovered that the most intelligent creatures on Earth, kilo for kilo, are turtles. I talk to them. I take them for walks. I play recordings of Wagnerian operas to make them happy. I'm selling you a machine to talk with the gods."

At that moment, I realized I was in a room with a genius who had gone completely off his rocker. Looney. Whacko. Crazy. Maybe it was from being alone too long. Maybe it was an effect from poison gas research during the Great War. But I knew I could not go back to Chicago with turtle cages.

Unfortunately, Frombeck had made an error. It was one of those life quirks that statistically is almost impossible. For you see, I am indeed a thug. I've murdered, extorted, etc. I'd killed my violent drunken father as a teenager. In all my life, I had only one pleasant memory that could bring a tear to my eye. My bedraggled mother came home one day with a present. She'd paid 50 cents at Woolworths and bought me a pet.

A little box turtle. It came in a small cardboard box with holes punched in the lid for air. I loved that turtle. I'd named him Binky. I'd killed my father because he'd come home drunk and threw the turtle against the wall. All those turtles with wires in their tiny heads made the tears flow down my scarred face.

I calmly pulled out my very noisy Colt .45 from the holster and shot Frombeck right between the eyes. I then spent hours gently removing the wire electrodes from each turtle, dabbing iodine on the wounds, and setting them free in the surrounding jungle. Frombeck's body wound up at the bottom of the ocean. A snack for the sharks.

I steer the boat toward the mainland with the new silent pistol in my pocket. The gang will find the new silent gun design worthy of $50,000. The bag of money is going into my safety deposit box for a rainy day. Sitting on my lap, my hand gently rests on a small cardboard box with air holes poked in the lid.

Jake "The Hammer" Hurley is a rising member of the South Side Gang. He and his compatriots have interests in breweries, gambling, and protection services. "The Hammer" specializes in the collection of debts for his organization. Capt. Benson of the twelfth police precinct stated that "Jake is a thug's thug. A man who you'd best not cross. Unfortunately we can't prove a thing. Witnesses disappear."

Jake spends evenings escorting Yolanda, an exotic dancer at the Orchid Club. He also anonymously contributes cash to building a new reptile building at the City Zoo.

Michael Rettig is a left handed, red headed only child who sees shapes in clouds no one else does. Once when fired from a job, instead of getting drunk, he went alone to a room and read Orwell's *1984* straight through. This is Mike's second story for *Mad Scientist Journal*. His first story was "Chuck the Alien." After an insanely stressful career as a stockbroker, Mike writes short stories. He's won a couple of short fiction contests and been a writing contest director. His writing critique group, "The Word Herd," meets frequently at the local Barnes and Noble.

NOTE ON THE LAW OF
THE EXCLUDED MIDDLE

An essay by Dr. Earnest Lee Lightweight,
as provided by Alan Meyrowitz

―――――――――

I had the privilege of delivering an invited talk to the 2014 Conference on Pushing the Boundaries and took that opportunity to speculate on the possibility that the Law of the Excluded Middle is not an immutable law after all. In its form most simply stated, adapted from Aristotle, the Law of the Excluded Middle asserts "Any statement must be either True or False, and can never be both." I provided some equations that were highly suggestive (at least to me, if not to the scientific establishment) that a region of space might be made to accommodate a contradiction to the Law, if that space were properly exposed to electromagnetic radiations.

As I could not entice funding from the usual research agencies and foundations, I proceeded as best I could with my own resources. Of necessity, a scientist working in his basement must make do with compromises. I purchased some items and scavenged others out of odd and ends. My efforts yielded a device consisting of a glass sphere, a meter in diameter, with field generators attached to its outside surface. Most importantly, the points of attachment were precisely dictated by my equations.

Two thermometers were included, side by side at the center of the sphere. They were connected to heating elements on the base supporting the sphere, and by computer I could direct the air in the sphere to be heated to precisely 90 degrees as determined by one thermometer, and to precisely 95 degrees as determined by the other. With all field generators active, I predicted that the temperature would register as both 90 degrees and 95 degrees simultaneously. Thus, the air inside the sphere would be at 90 degrees and not at 90 degrees, contradicting the Law of the Excluded Middle.

Regrettably, almost immediately after the heating elements were turned on, the sphere became a mass of glass fragments. Some of them littered the corners of my basement, but most piled around what had been the sphere's base. The catastrophe had been an implosion, not an explosion.

I could only conclude the air in the sphere had vanished, and moreover had vanished so quickly that in that instant, the glass could not support the sudden stress of the ambient air pressure impinging on it.

The logic of that soon became apparent. The universe would do what it must to preserve the Law, and so the simplest solution was for the air not to exist.

If you believe I immediately started to consider other designs for an experiment, you would be correct, but fortunately I also took the time to review my equations. I was startled to discover they not only allowed for an adjustment such as the air vanishing, in order for the universe to stay consistent with the Law, but any number of solutions were possible. Indeed both the air and the sphere itself might have ceased to exist, or my basement with all its contents including myself, or, as I believe, the whole of our universe might have vanished in an instant.

Preservation of the Law was not necessarily going for the simplest solution. It seemed a random choice to select implosion from among the possibilities, a fortunate choice considering the implications of the others.

So I must conclude no further experimentation can be risked. I will not be publishing any elaboration of my preliminary equations, nor will I be suggesting any further exploration of this topic. I strongly urge the scientific community to do the same.

P. S. The whereabouts of Dr. Toby Flakey, with whom I collaborated early on, should be determined. I fear he may not be inclined to the same research constraints as I.

Earnest Lee Lightweight received his Doctorate in Animal Husbandry from Miskatonic University in 1992. He credits his insights into physics to his keen observations of billiard ball behavior, all documented in his book *Revolution in Physics*. However, publication efforts were suspended upon learning his ideas substantially duplicated those of Sir Isaac Newton. Undaunted, Dr. Lightweight aggressively pursued experimental research. The U. S. Patent Office notes that he holds the record for the highest number of rejected patent applications submitted by one person. Still, Dr. Lightweight has collected his ideas in the draft of a new book, *The Virtue of Perseverance.*

Alan Meyrowitz retired in 2005 after a career in computer research. His creative writing has appeared in *California Quarterly, Eclectica, Existere, Front Range Review, The Literary Hatchet, The Nassau Review, Schuylkill Valley Journal, Shroud, The Storyteller,* and others. In 2012 and 2015, the Science Fiction Poetry Association nominated his poems for a Dwarf Star Award.

IT WON'T COST YOU A CENT
A letter by J. Julian Watson,
as provided by his cousin, Dana Mele

———————

Dear Family and Friends,

Happy holidays from the Watson family! As always, this December delivers swirling snow, crowded malls, and another annual update from Julian, Molly, Hunter, and Tesla. It's been a year, and so much has happened. Hunter is halfway through his first year of kindergarten, and loving it. Molly has been promoted at the Post Office! As for me, exciting things are on the horizon.

First, I have finally managed to shimmy out of the corporate noose. After another round of layoffs at CrypTech, I had the pleasure of turning in my badge and collecting a generous severance package, which will keep us clothed and fed for another month at least.

To tell the truth, it's the best thing that's ever happened to me. I'm finally free to pursue my own interests and engage in cutting edge research and development that allows me to contribute to the betterment of the world. I couldn't be more pleased with the results so far.

You will remember, of course, that incident at last year's Christmas party. I do apologize. I allowed myself one too many glasses of Nana's delicious eggnog, which does little to improve my personality. It got me thinking. If alcohol has such a detrimental effect on human behavior, shouldn't there be a drink that has the opposite effect? Not a chemical compound that only benefits people with mental diseases, but a healthy, naturally occurring substance that can improve mood and behavior for all of mankind? Don't we, as a human race, deserve such a thing? Think of all the evil that would be eliminated from the world, if only there were some easy way to stifle selfishness, repressed animosity, and uninhibited impulsivity, which I have determined are the three main behavioral results of excessive alcohol consumption.

If so, the human race is in for a real treat. I have spent the last year creating and perfecting such a formula. It is 100% natural, derived from plants you might find in your own backyard, depending upon where you happen to live (it's unlikely that anyone lives in both a desert and arctic climate, but who knows? The universe is a big place with infinite possibilities). It is rich in vitamins and minerals and only 20 calories per serving. Best of all, *it works.*

Molly, Hunter, and I have been on a steady diet of oatmeal, tomato juice, and Azure (so named because of its delightful hue) for the past six months and have never felt better. No more squabbles over the remote. No more struggles over who takes the garbage out. Did I mention that Molly was promoted to manager five months ago? I think I did! After previously being put on probation twice for aggressive behavior. And little Hunter, who used to crawl around on the ground, barking and pretending to be a dog whenever spoken to? Now he speaks, in plain English, to his teachers, his classmates, and to us. As for me, I haven't touched a drop of alcohol in almost a year. All thanks to Azure.

If it sounds like this holiday update has turned into something of a sales pitch, fear not! I would like to offer free samples to all of our friends and family, to share this wonderful discovery with all of you. It won't cost you a cent. I do ask that you spread the word amongst all of your own friends, families, and co-workers. I've enclosed a packet for you to sample. All you do is sprinkle the powder into a glass of water, stir vigorously, and drink it down. I find it has a pleasant, potable flavor with a nontoxic aftertaste. Don't worry if your tongue starts to tingle or goes numb. This wears off within an hour after consumption.

Hey, if you're worried, try first on your pet! Tesla loves it so much he refuses to touch his dog food nowadays. His tongue is permanently stained blue and he is the happiest, most docile canine on the block. If you remember, we were previously sued in civil court by our neighbors for nuisance due to his little biting problem.

Now our neighbors are just as hooked on Azure as we are, and Tesla is as welcome in their pool as he is in his own doghouse.

Hold on, you're thinking. What's the catch? The only catch is that once you try it, you'll never want to drink anything else, or for that matter, eat anything else. Again, this can be solved by forcing yourself to consume a measured amount of oatmeal and tomato juice each day, or a simple mash of grains and vegetables. All I ask is that you try it once. And that you serve it once to each family member, friend, and person that you have access to. Cousin Maria, try mixing Azure into your delicious matzo ball soup at the diner! Uncle Hal, why not provide Azure instead of Gatorade at your next bible study group? Aunt Tina, consider serving Azure to your students with some carrot sticks as a healthy snack. Before you get caught up in some silly ethical dilemma about feeding unsuspecting minors a non-FDA approved beverage with psychoactive properties, remember that it's good for you. 100 percent all natural, organic, and GMO free. Once you try it, you'll be hooked, and so will they.

As if that weren't good enough news, I would like to extend to you an exciting new business opportunity. Once you've developed a taste for Azure (and it only takes one sip), I know you'll want to share it with everyone you know. You can, and even better, at a profit. After careful consideration, I have decided against mass distribution (no thank you, corporate greed!) and plan to rely on word of mouth and a network of reliable, independent entrepreneurs to spread the word, and taste, of Azure. With every sale (please do remember to provide a free sample to every consumer before asking for any money) of Azure, you will retain 20% of the profits, at no cost to you. In time, and with the drastic reduction in household expenditures that comes along with a minimal diet and complete contentment, you will be able to quit your day job and rely entirely on your Azure earnings, with no decrease in quality of life.

Well, that's about all that's going on with us. We've had a phenomenal year, thanks to the selfish misers at CrypTech, a mild hurricane season, and a certain blue powder that has changed our lives forever. I can't wait to hear how much you all love it.

Warmly,
Julian, Molly, Hunter, and Tesla

P.S. As you were reading this, tiny particles of Azure have been seeping into your system through your fingertips. Azure makes a delightful royal blue ink, and adds a tasteful dash of color to stationary. Aren't you feeling much better already?

———

J. Julian Watson is a chemist and entrepreneur. He holds an A.B. from Harvard University and a Ph.D. from Massachusetts Institute of Technology. Dr. Watson is the youngest living recipient of the MacArthur genius grant, and is the former head of molecular research at CrypTech, Inc. His areas of specialization include computational biophysical chemistry and design and analysis of drugs. He is passionate about gardening, playing the ukulele, and musical theater. He lives in Greenville, New York, with his lovely wife Molly, his son Hunter, and his dog, Tesla.

———

Dana Mele is a writer and attorney currently located in a remote corner of the Catskill mountains. She has a B.A. from Wellesley College and is presently a student at the UCLA Extension Writer's Program. Her fiction and academic writing have appeared in *101 Words* and the *Syracuse Journal of Science and Technology*. She spends her time drafting wills and writing elegies for fallen logs, chasing her toddler in endless concentric circles, and avoiding bears.

LETTER OF RECOMMENDATION
FOR MINION BALROG
A letter by H. K. Ludwig, as provided by Shane Landry

To whom it may concern:

I had the privilege of supervising Balrog for seven years and, in fact, created him. He was the Security Specialist for Level Zero, where Patient Zeros, doomsday weapons, and government conspiracy-grade devices are kept. The position was fast paced and demanding, yet Balrog performed his duties with enthusiasm, dedication, and a keen attention to detail. In short, he was the consummate professional, always ready to smash, blast, and devour.

Balrog possesses a host of skills, qualities, and specialized knowledge that you will no doubt find useful. He is adept at stopping breaches in lab security. I vividly remember the day when Balrog stopped an out of control mutated simian-mantis hybrid that quickly grew to three stories tall. Despite a clear disadvantage in reach and body mass, Balrog completed the task without complaint and single-handedly contained the situation. That is exactly the sort of initiative and adherence to corporate mission statement that any company would benefit from.

His regenerative qualities stand out as his finest. When I say he stopped the mutation single-handedly, I mean literally. Balrog gives of himself readily when corporate needs far exceed the ability of lesser minions to meet them. More than once, he gave up his own hand to fuel the biomass generators. And while regrowth of a limb might have dampened the enthusiasm of a lesser minion, he still chanted "Balrog SMAAASH" with the terrifying volume I have learned to expect from him as a result of his dedication to quality fear-mongering.

Balrog has a working knowledge of the delicate insides of organic opponents and a keen understanding of the weak points within mechanical constructs. If your company ever decides to engage in corporate warfare, Balrog is an excellent point man, capable of designing an improvised entrance at a moment's notice.

I would absolutely rehire Balrog if given the opportunity. I am proud to have worked with him all these years. As his creator, I would almost go as far to say I am proud to be his father, but sociopathic tendencies brought about by a genius intellect and a childhood of perpetual bullying impede me from doing so. If you have any questions or would like to discuss his abundant qualifications in further detail, I will make myself available at any time. Thank you for considering Balrog as a minion in your mad science. You will not find a finer Security Specialist anywhere in this dimension.

Regards,
H. K. Ludwig
CEO and CTO of HK Industries

P.S. If your company is foolish enough to test your pitiful resources against the might of HK Industries, I would consider it a professional courtesy if you did not send Balrog for at least 90 days after hire. Such an act would represent a conflict of interest.

H. K. Ludwig was born in Cortex, Alabama. He endured a socially isolated childhood as a result of his clinically diagnosed superior intellect. At age seven, he built his first minion and discovered people are more tractable when their house is on fire. He later founded HK Industries with a core focus of custom minion development and accessories. The inevitable success brought about by his peerless brilliance led to the acquisition of many inferior companies specializing in other technologies, ranging from freeze-grenade snow cones to android girlfriend vending machines. He currently lives at the top of the food chain.

———————

Shane Landry was born on the East Coast where driving is a full contact sport. He has a degree in Applied Physics and spent 13 months as a research assistant in the South Pole, Antarctica. When not writing, he conditions his body and mind for the zombie apocalypse, brews beer, and plays guitar so poorly the instrument filed a restraining order. Authorities report he is currently teaching English in Japan. You can visit his website at www.shanelandrybooks.com.

CONSTRUCTING THE PROVABLY COMPLETE LIBRARY

An essay by V. Cardigan, as provided by Emma Tonkin

Abstract

The theoretical concept of a provably complete library, generated by an infinitely parallelised random process, is well-known. In this article, I report on the results of a sample implementation of Borel's well-known "typing monkey" thought experiment. Through analysis and evaluation of our practical findings, I identify best practices, issues encountered, and potential future developments in the field.

Introduction

Ever since the publication of Émile Borel's contribution to the field of modern librarianship in his well-known 1913 article, "Mécanique Statistique et Irréversibilité," the construction of a *provably complete library* (PCL) has been tantalisingly close to humanity's grasp.

Borel's pioneering vision described the employment of an infinitely large number of "singes dactylographes," usually rendered into English as "typing monkeys," each of which would generate a unique text on his or her individual typewriter. Although the majority of such texts would naturally contain nothing but gibberish, a small subset would consist of all existing (and possible) works of literature. The aggregate works of an infinite set of monkeys would therefore far exceed the reach of copyright libraries, institutions that are entitled to a copy of every book ever published in the host nation. Such a library would also contain valid textual encodings of all possible binary formats, software packages, scripts, and multimedia works. The PCL is a provably complete textual, image, multimedia, and software library.

Borel's work has generally been dismissed as purely theoretical due to the difficulties inherent in the practical construction of an infinite dataset. In particular, although contemporary computing platforms are able to simulate a series of individual typing monkeys, they do not permit the simulation of the requisite infinite set of typing monkeys in a realistic period of time. In the past, parallelization has failed to significantly relieve this difficulty. The best parallel architectures commercially available today cannot provide the infinite parallelism required by Borel's *Gedankenexperiment.*

A practical application of infinitely parallel computing

Last year, we in the Information and Library Services department were pleased to learn of the eighteen-billion-pound development of a new infinitely parallel quantum computing (IPQC) facility within our university. This construction made extensive use of existing facilities provided by the Physics Department's very high energy physics research group and was to be operated by the cryptography research group, a collaboration between the Schools of Computing and Mathematics.

Whilst I am not an expert on the system's theoretical underpinnings, it is my understanding that, although a quantum computer only requires a single universe in which to operate, this facility electively transcends the limitations of our universe by breaking through into an infinitely parallel local multiverse. Hence, it allows the programmer to draw upon a true infinite-dimensional Hilbert computational space. Metaphorically, the IPQC facility can be viewed as an uplink to the wireless networking endpoint of the monolithic high-performance computing facility provided by our local multiverse.

The system's potential as an exploitable resource for the Information and Library Services department was immediately clear. Under the leadership of our department head, Dr McTavish, we therefore made a successful funding application to the

University. In this, we drew attention to the fact that the IPQC was the first system in existence capable of underpinning a real-life PCL. We additionally noted that such a library was more than simply a curiosity, since it would permit us to:

- **Reduce software licencing costs.** The full set of all possible software packages represented in the PCL, McTavish suggested, must include all software currently employed within the university and all possible equivalent packages and upgrades. We therefore proposed that the University identify and adopt alternative software packages drawn from within the PCL, phasing these into general use over the next three financial years. This was projected to save the University a significant sum of money in software licencing fees.

- **Eliminate academic journal subscriptions.** Despite the considerable savings achieved over the last decade by the University's librarians, our academic journal subscriptions draw on increasingly scarce financial resources. Whilst the copyright implications of automatically generated article duplicates are not entirely clear, no legal precedent could be found that prohibits their use.

- **Replace our existing institutional repository installation.** Since this library would contain all possible papers ever to be published by all staff members, it would avoid any need for manual deposit of preprints by the authors, thus representing a significant cost and time saving on the part of our librarians. Furthermore, since academics and researchers could simply search the PCL for their future works, then submit them to relevant journals, it would also free considerable time for staff development and administrative activities. This time saving would permit us to provide better value for money to research funders, as well as increasing research impact and staff satisfaction.

McTavish also noted that the PCL could also, in principle, be used to identify and preemptively file patents, to beat others to publication, to preview unpublished papers, and so on. It was agreed with the University that, following the initial implementation phase, the relevant ethical issues would be explored by a focus group led by the University's School of Law.

Method and implementation

Using the IPQC, an entirely functional simulation of an infinite set of *singes dactylographes* was readily accomplished. Each of the resulting documents were stored across the multiverse in locally available storage. At this stage, in principle, our work had fulfilled the specifications laid down in the University's grant.

Following the completion of the document generation phase, it rapidly became clear to us that the storage of digital information is not the key challenge. Although necessary, the storage of an infinite set of documents is not sufficient. For usability and accessibility reasons, it is also necessary to support practical methods of searching for and accessing information.

Ideally, I hoped that we might develop application programming interfaces able to provide local developers with access to the PCL, so that the Complete Library service could be queried via the University intranet. To do this, we would first need to develop an infinitely parallel search algorithm capable of operating within infinite-dimensional Hilbert space. This was a daunting task.

However, Professor Whitloaf (Chair of *studia generalia*) suggested to me that there was no need to manually generate this algorithm. Since the necessary algorithm was itself textual, it would already be available somewhere in our PCL dataset. Therefore, we just had to create a bootstrap algorithm capable of identifying and extracting valid sorting algorithms, using straightforward unit testing of all materials within the Library. We could then search the Library using an algorithm retrieved directly from the Library itself. This example of "eating our own dogfood" seemed a parsimonious and efficient solution, which struck the team as both elegant and achievable. We therefore designed and ran a bootstrap algorithm, which would identify, extract and list compatible sorting algorithms from the Library's dataset.

Results and discussion

An optimal sorting and indexing algorithm was successfully

retrieved within milliseconds. I provide a listing for this algorithm, which according to our analysts is suitable for use on an infinite-dimensional Hilbert space (see Listing A). We then received another two hundred and fifty thousand equivalent algorithms within the next minute, a rate that has subsequently continued unabated, forcing us to conclude that our bootstrap software contains a bug.

Dr Leona Butler, a postdoctoral researcher who conducted a thorough analysis of the returned data, observed that the set of valid indexing algorithms would itself be infinitely large. We were disturbed by this finding. Although the IPQC offers infinitely parallel processing capacity, meaning that it took very little time to unit-test appropriately sized objects within the system, the finite rate of intra-universe input-output serialisation remains a significant bottleneck. Specifically, bandwidth limitations resulting from the present high-energy particle physics uplink implementation limit input-output capacity to under a hundred megabits per second on average. Unfortunately, we had not thought to build a system interrupt into the bootstrap algorithm, so we are unable to halt the ongoing listing process.

Conclusion

We have successfully developed a Provably Complete Library facility and tested it by retrieving algorithms suitable for information indexing and retrieval. However, we are unable to implement the resulting algorithms on the University's IPQC, as it is now projected to continue broadcasting an infinitely large number of subtle variants of this indexing algorithm until the end of time. We have proposed that a second IPQC be funded, but as we are aware of only one suitable local multidimensional Hilbert space in which to compute, this option is entirely impractical unless someone figures out how to press the reset button on the multiverse.

Although I have not been able to make the PCL available to university faculty or students, I propose that our result be viewed as a concrete and successful contribution to a separate field, notably, the Search for Extraterrestrial Intelligence (SETI) programme. Any future species within range of the local multiverse with access to an adequate level of technology, and which chooses to connect to and analyse the output of the computational Hilbert space that our realities share, will discover the eternal beacon that the human race has left behind.

Very little future work is now conceivable in this domain. It is a shame, of course, that our first and only information-retrieval operation on this unique and irreplaceable resource has dropped it into an irretrievably infinite loop. Still, as Professor Whitloaf says, it could've been worse. At least we got it working. Once.

Acknowledgements

This work was carried out with the support of the University and the European Union. A full list of relevant grants is published in Appendix 2.

Biography

Vera Cardigan received a Master's in Library and Information Science from the University of the West of Peterborough and is a member of the International Library Society's Experimental Librarianship Interest Group. She is employed as a senior librarian at St Alexander's University College, formerly Oxford Agricultural Polytechnic.

Emma Tonkin is an engineer with a PhD in computer science and a lingering fascination with classical studies. She is employed in a research project in the sub-basement of a University building. She likes to write fiction and sometimes even manages it on purpose.

THE STATE OF MAD SCIENCE, 2016

A speech by Professor T.D. McClure, MPhD, President of the Mad Scientists of America, presented by Laura Roberts

———

Dr. Evil, Mr. Vice President, Members of the International Scientific Community, my enemies, my co-conspirators, my fellow Mad Scientists:

The State of Mad Science in 2016 is a precarious one, despite our many advances, and thus I come to you today to report back on our successes, our failures, and our plans for the future. Not just for the next year, but for the next five years, the next ten years, and beyond. I believe we must focus on the future, rather than reverting to missions of the past, because the Mad Scientists of America must continue to grow, embrace change, and set an example for the twisted hearts and addled minds of the next generation of Mad Scientists.

Mad Science has been through big changes before, and we have always come out swinging. Whether we were being crushed by fascist do-gooders, removed from tenured positions at prestigious universities, or simply tarred and feathered in the press by those who misunderstood our mission, we always continued to forge ahead, to do our work in secret, and to think up new ways to demonstrate our own brand of evil genius.

The time has come, not to cower from the light, but to embrace the darkness—and to fire up the Tesla Coil! (Applause.)

My fellow Mad Scientists, here is just a short list of the things we have accomplished in the past year:

- In the field of archaeology, we managed to convince the world that our spectacularly realistic bone fragments, dumped in the depths of a cave in South Africa, actually belong to "homo nalendi," a new species of humanoid ancestor. The non-mad scientific community is still buzzing about the import of this discovery, and they believe they've discovered a new branch on the human family tree, when in fact they are playing right into our hands as we set up our most cruel and cunning prank yet. Phase 2 of this project begins soon, so be sure to subscribe to our mailing list in order to follow each new twist and turn.

- Working closely with both mad and non-mad scientists in China, we have successfully inserted DNA from a woolly mammoth into the cells of a modern elephant. Though the non-mad scientists have been informed that this experiment was a failure, our mad brethren have secretly moved the resulting Modern Mammoth to one of our underground lairs for safekeeping. (Special shout-out to Dr. Evil for providing his volcano sanctuary for more in-depth research.) Project Mammoth Mayhem is set to debut in Spring 2017, with plenty of hair-raising fun in store.

- While the non-mad scientists of NASA brought forth their discovery of water on the surface of Mars, highlighting the accomplishment in a mainstream Hollywood movie that shall remain nameless, we mad scientists have also made exciting discoveries on the red planet! Indeed, while the world fawned over NASA's findings, we secretly maneuvered Curiosity (the Mars Rover) to a remote hollow on the surface of the planet to achieve additional imaging of a rare protozoa with a thirst for blood. We are nearly certain it was this species that ultimately wiped out the people of Mars, and that sent any survivors scurrying for the cold comforts of space, desperate for revenge. It is armed with this information that we have been contacting alien life in the vicinity of the 666 Nebula and proposing the final outline of a full-scale War of the Worlds set on the red planet. There is quite a lag in terms of our current communications with the people of 666 Nebula, but early indicators point to signs of agreement with this plan. The war is currently set to begin June 6th, 2017, if all goes according to plan. Stay tuned as we continue to negotiate with Hollywood for a space thriller of our own! (Evil laughter.)

- Along with our plans for interplanetary domination, the

discovery of the brightest galaxy in the universe has given us new information that should help fuel our ongoing evil schemes. A supermassive black hole at the center of this inordinately bright universe (dubbed "WISE J224607.57-052635.0" by the media, but known simply as "The Darkness" to our scientists) is key to our reign of terror, as it is powerful enough to pull in everything from Death Stars to Starkillers with its mighty lust for fuel. At only 12.5 billion light years away, we have updated our timelines accordingly; please see the new plans on our website.

- Finally, dozens of new evil species have been discovered and documented in the Eastern Himalayas, including the elusive Yeti, the Abominable Snowman, and the Lesser Neanderthal Cave Chimp, whose razor-sharp teeth have proven excellent additions to our genetic modification program.

We continue to make great strides in all areas of mad robotics and AI, mad marine biology, and mad chemistry, despite the usual drawbacks of working within the socially accepted norms of the non-mad scientific community.

While non-mad geniuses like Neil deGrasse Tyson and Bill Nye continue to undermine our progress in the mad sciences, we too seek to become household names. And while they seek to spread a message of science as the great equalizer, bringing peace through technology, we shall continue our mission to conquer the planet—and the galaxy—one step at a time, with STEAM (Science, Technology, Engineering, Arts, Mathematics) programs in grade and middle schools across America, blossoming into explorations into the mad sciences in high schools, and continuing on to full-fledged Mad Science Studies with MBS (Mad Bachelor of Science) and MMS (Mad Master of Science) degrees at the college level.

We seek to be known not only for the creativity of our schemes, but also for the caliber of our weapons! (Applause.)

Is there, indeed, any part of the mad science community into which we have not yet stuck a bony, probing finger? I am here to proudly tell you that the answer to this rhetorical question is *no*. In fact, it is *hell no!* Can I get a *hell no?!* (Applause. Pause for chanting of "hell no.")

So you see, my fellow Mad Scientists, it is neither the wrack and ruin of our economy nor the failure of our members to rise to the occasion that has concluded my fourth year on such a high note. No, today I stand before you as the President of the Mad Scientists of America, humbly requesting your endorsement for yet another term. Together, I believe we can achieve the goals of this society, and that we can finally rise above the nonsensical restrictions of the non-mad scientific community, to burst forth like a supernova of evil genius with our death rays and mind-control devices, rallying every man, woman, child, and monster to join in our plots, our schemes, and our ultimate domination of the universe.

Alone, we are but mortals, prone to death and failure. But together? Together, we can do anything. In the words of Napoleon Bonaparte: "Impossible is a word found only in the dictionary of fools."

Thus I ask you: Are we fools, or are we Mad Scientists? I believe we all know the answer to that one. (Applause.)

My fellow Mad Scientists, I salute you. Thank you, may Baal bless you, and good night.

———

T. D. McClure holds an MPhD (Mad PhD) from Harvard, and currently serves as the President of the Mad Scientists of America. In addition to being an incredibly sought-after keynote speaker on the subjects of mad science and evil ingenuity in times of crisis, McClure has also won a Mad Nobel Prize, the National Medal of Mad Science, and a Profile in Courage Award. You may also remember McClure as the inventor of the MindRay 2.1, a mind-control device that has threatened both national and international security on a broad scale. His further exploits are detailed at http://Buttontapper.com.

———

Laura Roberts can leg-press an average-sized sumo wrestler, has nearly been drowned off the coast of Hawaii, and tells lies for a living. She is the founding editor of *Black Heart Magazine*, the San Diego Chapter Leader for the Nonfiction Authors Association, and publishes whatever strikes her fancy at Buttontapper Press. She currently lives in an Apocalypse-proof bunker in sunny SoCal with her artist husband and their literary kitties, and can be found online at Buttontapper.com.

FICTION

MIXED
By Saffron Grey

Ty Salvo always had the curiosity and intelligence to do whatever he wanted. He earned all the high expectations and praises. No one knew that better than I did. I, who followed him around like an assistant. We'd taken different paths, but we still found ourselves in the same examination room of a Kyoto City hospital. I, the patient. He, the doctor. I wondered how well we would play our roles, how far we would get.

"Caprina," he said softly, "I *am* truly sorry."

I waved him off. "It's not like you chopped it off. A freak accident—no big deal."

"No big deal?" It was like we were five years old again with the way he was looking at me, gearing up to scold me. "Caprina—"

"Relax, Ty. Just tell me what I'm supposed to do about the infection." It was a small one, my skin reacting to the chemicals they'd used to close up the wound and smooth out the broken radius and ulna. I'd just lost my hand five hours ago, and I believed anything rushed wouldn't work well.

Ty had a difficult time looking away from my stump. "It's just one pill. The infection will clear up in 12 hours or so. Drink plenty of water."

"That's it? No 'two pills a day' or something?"

A smile managed to break through his worried face. "Things are a little different up here."

"Oh. Right—" Kyoto City: a tech and medical discovery *goldmine* for the better part of the world in the 22nd century. I could never afford a doctor up here.

"Do you feel any pain at the wrist?" he asked, reading something on his screen.

"My wrist is kind of, um, gone."

He glanced at me before frowning at the screen. "Oh, my apologies. I didn't know the image was cut off—" He closed his eyes and pressed his lips together in a small fit of frustration. "My apologies again."

I giggled at all the eggshells he was avoiding. "You talk so formal now." The pale blue lab coat accented the brown of his skin.

"Part of the environment, I guess." The chuckle from when he was a kid had a deeper resonance now, but it was still the same. "A lot of my peers are from Suriname."

"Anyone I would know?"

"Um—" Ty thought really hard. "Remember Shana? She's a nurse now."

"Eh—no." Too many kids had filtered through the orphanage to remember names. Maybe I knew Shana, but not her name.

Ty turned off his screen and folded it away. "I'll go get the medication." He glanced back at the stump before leaving the room. I removed both my arms from the table.

It was too bare without him. The walls were too clean. There seemed to be no sort of smell in the room. You could go nowhere in Suriname without smelling *something*. The absence of it was unsettling. Kyoto City was too pristine. How could it not be? It didn't have to deal with the faeries the way Suriname did.

The door slid open at Ty's return. He held a petri dish and a cup of water. "So where do you work now?" He took his seat opposite the table. "What do you do?"

"I'm a key coder for the dome."

His eyes widened. "All the way out *there*? Isn't it dangerous?"

I waved my stump. "Rarely, actually. They don't always make it through the wall."

"How did you end up there?"

"They needed people with good memories," I shrugged, reaching for the petri dish. "It pays really well for a reason, though." Ty removed the lid of the petri dish for me, and I took out the pill, popping it into my mouth.

He pushed the cup toward me. "How long have you been there?"

I chugged the whole cup, the pill going down smoothly. "Two years now."

"Really?"

"*Yeah*," I laughed. "This was the first attack they'd had in *three*. The faeries are learning, their frequencies slowly adapting. You didn't hear this from *me*, but—"

"Ah." Ty nodded at a corner of the room as he stood up. "Well, that's all you need from me, *Ms. Kapoor*." He was cautious. "You're well enough to go home. You'll have to make an appointment with your primary doctor in a couple of days, of course."

"No problem." I got to my feet and stretched. "I could use a few days off."

He led us to the door and I followed him into the hallway. "Days off? You're still going to work there?"

"Of course! I don't want to lose my job. I'll be moved to a different sector, farther from the wall where I don't have to be as fast, but ... Ty, *come on*."

He shook his head. "My ap—I'm sorry. It just baffles me."

We sidestepped around doctors and patients going by. "I got what I got, and I don't need a lot." He smiled at our counselor's old saying. "It was really nice seeing you, knowing you're doing well."

"I'd say the same, but ... *goodness*—you lost a hand."

I looked at my stump, which now ended two inches below where my wrist used to be. "I was right-handed."

That startled a laugh out of Ty. "I'm—I'm sorry! I know it's not funny—"

"That's why I said it—*relax*. Don't you know how to do that anymore?"

He sighed back into seriousness. "Not much time to do that here." We were reaching the end of the hallway that led into the lobby. I would go all the way back to Suriname, and Ty would probably get back to work. He stopped us, and we moved closer to the wall. "I wish we could talk a little longer—catch up after these past what, five years?"

"I think it's been six."

"Six whole years ... I spent most of them buried in books."

"Must've annoyed your girlfriend," I fished.

He laughed and looked away, eyes on the shiny linoleum. "No, no girlfriends. None that stuck around, anyway. No time for dates."

"That's too bad. Most girls are encouraged to date doctors."

"They should try and *be* one. No time for socializing. I bet coding for the walls must be exciting."

I laughed then. "Eight hours spent in front of screens changing codes. I don't know what the girl sitting next to me even looks like."

"But it's important work," he said seriously, "keeping the walls secure from the faeries. That hole out there should close up soon, no?"

"Eh—" It wasn't really meant for public ears that the holes in the ground weren't getting smaller. More and more faeries roamed around the walls that surrounded Suriname (the outer city) and Kyoto City (the inner). I looked to the clock. "I gotta get going. Need to report to my supervisor in the morning."

"Wait—" He reached for my left arm, even though I hadn't started moving yet. "I get off in a few minutes. Want to go get something to eat?"

I didn't want to seem too eager. Getting to spend more time with Ty tonight hadn't seemed like a possibility ten minutes ago. "I need to catch the last bus."

"I can give you a ride after."

"All the way out to Suriname?"

He made a face. "You act like I wasn't born there."

"In that lab coat and new way of talking, anyone could forget. But, sure."

Ty smiled so brightly I remembered why I always followed him around. "Great. Wait for me in the lobby. I know a great place to eat."

"Okay, but keep in mind that I'm low on funds. Nothing too fancy."

He lightly punched me in the arm. "This will be my treat. Don't worry about *anything*."

~

No one was in the lobby, so I had no one to stare at my handless right arm. My sweater sleeve draped at the end, making me feel like a child in a grownup's clothes.

The silent telescreen in the corner showed a stern-faced reporter. The news ticker on the bottom read "World leaders to meet June 21st, 2116, regarding 3 newly discovered 'faerie rips' in

Africa, Indonesia, and New Zealand." They followed it with security footage from the walls: colorful monsters with long claws scratching at the codes zipping in front of their faces.

The faerie problem was growing every day, no matter how much we tried to hide it. At least most of the larger cities had their walls coded. Now all that was left was the smaller areas. We kept losing those to the holes opening up in the ground.

Walls of code, specifically designed to jar the frequencies the faeries seemed to operate on. A 40-year-long struggle was being reduced as more and more areas acquired coding equipment to erect the miles of coded wall. Parts of entire countries had been lost to these faerie creatures—beautiful from a distance, but monsters of teeth and claw once they were close. As for where they came from—

"Ready to go?"

Ty interrupted my thoughts. He was out of his coat, now in a jacket over black pants. "I know," he said. "I look less professional."

I got up and followed him to the front entrance. "You actually look more relaxed."

He made a one-time "Hm" that was followed by silence as we walked to the parking lot. Very few people were out, only one or two cars driving by. I'd thought nights in Kyoto City would be loud and colorful, every night some kind of event happening on every street. Prosperous people enjoying their safety and comfort.

"Is it always this quiet?" I asked.

"Around a hospital, yes." Ty stopped us in front of a sleek black car. "Downtown is where the action is, but we're not going there tonight." He pulled out his key and pressed the button, the lights of the car blinking twice.

"Oh?" Not *tonight*, but *another* night? Dating Ty would be problematic.

"We're going someplace I like to go to relax." We got inside his car and he started it, the seat beginning to warm itself.

"Is it stressful being a doctor here?"

"I shouldn't complain, really." He pulled the car onto the street and we sped up. "The injuries that usually come in are minor. Amputees are rare, but we're trained for almost anything."

"Not a lot of dangerous jobs in the city."

"No. Do you like being a wall coder?"

"Yes and no. Yes because it feels like important work—creating the walls that protect us from the faeries. It's tedious on the surface, but the offices have screens that watch the perimeter, and it's sort of satisfying seeing your work repel those monsters." I shuddered. "Other than their purple or green skin colors, pointy ears, and crazy claws and teeth, they look pretty similar to humans. It's creepy."

"What about the 'no' part?"

"The toll it has on you physically. Sitting or standing, we spend most of the day at a desk facing a screen. We wear special glasses so the glare of the screen doesn't ruin our eyes. Really, the only interesting part is memorizing the next line of code to be used later. That's about the only interesting stress. That and, well, watching the faeries."

He turned a corner and we started to mix in with other cars. "How did the faeries break through?"

I laughed. "Someone fell asleep at their desk and their coding stopped, creating a gap in the wall. The faeries found it and jumped through, swarming in like ants. The control center doesn't want people to know this, but they've got *abilities*."

"What kind of—"

"It'd be called telekinesis or whatever by the scientific community, but it's not just the manipulation of objects. They can bend electricity or water or the dirt around them—control them. A lot of the folks in Suriname call it magic."

Ty laughed. "Magic's not real."

"Obviously. But you really had to be there to see it."

"So you saw them?"

I nodded. "In the flesh. I was in the back of the room, though, so I wasn't very close. One of them—a tall one, maybe a male or something—he jammed his clawed hand into one of the rotors for our generators, tore out the fan blades, and sent them flying. He didn't *throw* them, though. He ripped them out, tossed them into the air, and they just flew. I didn't see the one coming in my direction—too busy falling back as everyone rushed to the door— but the next thing I knew—" I held up my stump, the undeniable evidence.

The car slowed down. "You must've been terrified."

"I *was*, up until I lost the hand. I probably passed out, since I don't remember leaving the room. I woke up in the ambulance, after the emergency crews had come in to handle the faeries that had come in. Someone in another room had taken up the code for the section and closed it off. Safe to say the one who fell asleep was fired."

Ty maneuvered the car into a parking lot, reversing into a space. When he turned it off, he sat quietly for a few seconds, staring at the building in front of us. "I seriously can't imagine it. I've seen footage of them on the news, but—"

"They're much bigger up close," I chuckled.

He looked at me. "For someone who lost a hand to them, you're handling it pretty well."

I shrugged. "Maybe it still hasn't hit me."

"And you're not angry or sad or—?"

"I don't know yet, really. I'm—" My stomach rumbled. "I'm kind of hungry now."

Ty looked more at ease and smiled. "Let's go inside."

The place wasn't as fancy as I had expected—and I was relieved because I was still dressed in my work clothes, my jacket the cleanest thing on me. Ty found us a booth by a window, the lights of cars streaming by. I didn't recognize anything on the menu and had Ty order for me.

I couldn't call this a date. This was two old friends catching up after one of them got a hand cut off. No big deal. I'd memorized it all and then some.

"Caprina," he said after a few minutes of silence.

I liked hearing him say my name; he said it much nicer than other people. "Hmm?"

"Other than catching up—which I'm glad we're able to do—I sort of had *another* reason for asking you here."

I nodded. "Okay."

"See, I have this friend—a *good* friend, a *doctor*, like me—and he kind of needs someone—"

"Are you thinking of setting us up?" The irony.

He laughed, at ease again. "No, actually, but I can always give it a shot."

"Continue." *Not* that I was interested in dating someone at the moment.

"This may sound really weird, but today might actually be your lucky day." He smiled when it was clear I didn't understand. "You see, my friend works with special cases similar to yours. He's been researching for a couple of years now, continuing the work of his predecessor. It's fairly new science, but we've—I mean, he's been trying to find test subjects—well, I mean, *patients* who meet the requirements. And, as of today, you meet a requirement."

"You mean—?" I held up my stump.

Ty nodded. "It's fairly new—a little radical, maybe, but Raj and I have been moving ahead with the next steps with much success."

"In plain English—what is it?"

He looked around the restaurant conspiratorially. "We're giving *amputees limbs back*."

I couldn't stop smiling at him, always going for the obvious and impossible. "If you and your friend are trying to put limbs back on people, it's not going to work on me. I have *no* idea where my hand ended up."

"We're actually going a little further than that."

Some kind of chill skittled down my spine. Even though I knew, I still felt like I didn't—believing my own role. "I have a wild guess, but I think I'm wrong."

"I don't think you're wrong," he said quietly. "I know it sounds crazy, but doctors have already transplanted limbs between humans, from dead and living donors. All it takes here is a little more studying, examinations and tests. In fact, depending on the appendages, we've already had successes."

"Successes?"

"Yes—three, to be precise. An entire arm, two legs, and an ear."

I was going to respond, though I had no words, but Ty and I leaned away from each other as our order was placed on the table. I was brought back to the restaurant, to the sound of utensils on plates and wordless chatter. I'd almost forgotten I was in Kyoto City. Ty was teaching me something, and again, I was lost in my idea of his mind. I needed to wrap my head around another thing. *I* was trying to lead him this time. Even now, I still doubted how well I could do it. He was always smarter than I was.

"There were almost no problems," he offered.

"Almost?"

"Well, the only complications were that the limbs didn't respond quickly to human blood. It took some time before our grafting process began to work. But we only had three subjects, three sets of tests, and *three* successes. You can't ask for better results than that."

"I'm not asking."

"You don't want a hand back?"

"It's not going to be a *human* hand."

"They have ten fingers—we have ten fingers. What difference does it make?"

Wow—what justification for monsters. "First of all, I haven't lived without my right hand long enough to get as desperate as you need me to be. As for what you and your friend are doing—it's *beyond* illegal."

Ty chuckled softly. "Everything's illegal at first, but as more and more people agree with it, laws will change. That's never stopped." He sat forward. "I wasn't expecting a 'yes' from the start, Caprina. Trust me—I felt the same way you did when Raj first told me. But his methods checked out. The science is sound. In fact, our methods are similar to the coded walls."

"How?"

"The frequencies they run on—how they communicate and how they heal—it's in their blood. It can still be boiled down to ones and zeroes. A little genetic and mathematical coding is all it takes. *Raj* is the biologist and surgeon—all the dirty work. I just write and check the numbers." He glanced at the groups of people in the restaurant. "The faeries are our enemies. We've grown up knowing that. What's wrong with taking advantage of them?"

"People would be disgusted at the *thought* of having a piece of *them attached* to their bodies forever."

"You don't seem so disgusted. You're eating just fine."

I glared at him. "I watch those things on screens every day. It's my *job* to keep them out. And here you are trying to bring them *in*." Besides, I'd missed lunch and dinner, and the food was very tasty. "What kind of people did you find willing to go for it?"

Ty sat back, sighing heavily. "The desperate kind. They didn't have the means to seek transplants. It isn't a matter of money either. Less and less people are choosing to be donors, so not a lot of spare parts are going around."

Not having what you need in Kyoto City? Never thought I'd hear that. "There's not a lot of danger here, is there?"

He shook his head. "What about Suriname? What's it like now?"

"The same. The closer to the edge you get, the dirtier and more unsettling it is. The faeries hover around the walls now, watching people and waiting for a hole to show up." The Kyoto City people wouldn't get it. Kyoto City was watched by humans—Suriname was watched by monsters. "How do you and Raj *get* them?"

He flashed a smile. "Once you're in our program, *then* you get to know."

"Do your subjects know?"

"Of course. They willingly participated and deserve to know where the parts come from. They're going to be living with them for the rest of their life."

"What do you do about the skin pigmentation?"

"The subjects are capable of covering them with makeup. Nothing to it."

"If your subjects are missing pieces, how do they explain suddenly having an arm, two legs, and an ear again?"

"Caprina, it's very easy to lie. Last I checked, there wasn't a shortage of donors in Suriname."

"So why didn't they just go down there and ask about donors?"

He smiled again, a softer one that lingered as he thought. "It's true. They could've gone and received a human arm, human legs, and a human ear. But first, there's the case of mismatching. Their bodies might reject the new parts and they'd have to start over. And then there's the fact that they went to *Suriname* and got spare *Suriname* parts. It's a struggle to deal with, but these people don't think much of us."

"And you're willing to *help* them?"

"Yes, if it means making a name for myself. It takes time to climb a mountain, Caprina, but I'm getting there soon."

~

It was a quiet drive to Suriname. If we said anything, it was about the road or the trees. It was difficult to stop thinking about his proposal, or the fact that he was going to continue with it— look for more volunteers—I made it a point not to acknowledge my stump.

Which was a problem. I'd reach up to move a lock of my hair out of my eyes but—oh right—no fingers. No right hand. It'd been easy to brush it off to others, but now that I sat in Ty's quiet car with my own thoughts, it was too noticeable.

"What did you think when you first saw them?" I said.

"When I first saw the faeries?"

I nodded. "Up close."

He scoffed. "I was scared—duh. It was already dead, but still. It was a male, taller than me and yet thinner. They're not really heavy. Did you know they had wings?"

"Yes, but we aren't supposed to tell people." We lived under a coded *dome*, not just a wall. Completely enclosed.

"Well, yeah. I helped Raj dissect those too. Despite carrying their weight, the wings didn't look engineered to carry such weight. It should be impossible for them to fly."

"Then how do they do it?"

"Raj has a few theories. One is that it's got something to do with the frequencies."

"It doesn't stop them from flying. Some have flown *into* the walls." Repeatedly.

"And then Raj has one that's got to do with magic."

I chuckled. "Magic's not real."

"I know, but that's what he calls it. However they fly, we can't compare it to birds." Ty drove slower as we entered some of the rural neighborhoods, the lights off. It was almost midnight. "If they work on frequencies, then it's got to be one different than the one they use to communicate or heal. A third one we've yet to crack. We haven't even paused to analyze their brains yet—we don't have the right equipment for that." We were reaching my street. "How good are you at the coding you do?"

"What, you want my help?"

He shrugged. "That offer's on the table too. Raj and I are having a hard time finding people we can trust, let alone with the smarts to help us."

I shook my head. "I've never been smart."

"There're all kinds of smarts. Having a good memory is a kind of smart too, especially if you know how to use it—and you use it every day—keeping Suriname and Kyoto City safe."

"Sounds more noble than it is."

"It *is* noble." He stopped the car outside my complex. "Listen, about what we talked about—"

"Ty—my *job* is to protect *and* keep secrets. I'm not breathing a word to anybody."

He reached into his pocket for his card holder, taking one out and handing it to me. "I'm not asking you to call me if you change your mind, but to call when you can hang out. I miss having a friend I can just relax with."

Only a phone number—no address. I opened the car door. "It was really good to catch up. I'll call soon, to hang out."

"I'd like that very much."

~

I'd stayed up all night with no results, doing all my own searching in case Ty or Raj got curious about me. I didn't know Ty would come back into my life and leave me stressed.

The number on his card was for his hospital office. I found his basic information on the hospital's servers and most of Kyoto City's residential information, but there was nothing that connected him to a person named Raj—if that was even his real name. All the modified scripts I'd memorized didn't find anything on Ty that suggested criminal activity—only a couple of paid parking tickets.

Ty was a curious person, but so was I. It was what made me follow him around, because he had the intelligence to satisfy our curiosity. Now that I had some skills of my own, I thought I could match him. But as I had improved, so had he.

Did I want a faerie hand? Hell no. Did I need to know how it was done? Hell yes.

I started combing hospital records, going back a year or two, and I searched for any patients missing an arm, two legs, or an ear. I was running a separate search over any accidents—faerie or otherwise—that would be devastating enough to cause such injuries. This second search should've failed anyway, because if anything big happened in Kyoto City, Suriname would've heard about it. But if it wasn't about faeries, we didn't care.

It was 6 am when I decided to take a break. I grew hungry again, and sleep caught up to me. I pushed my chair away from my three computer monitors—old ones the office had thrown away that I salvaged—and I rolled all the way to my fridge. I reached for the door handle, my stump bumping into it.

I kicked the chair away and stood up. This was something I'd have to get used to. The thrill of the search through Ty's Kyoto City life hadn't been an issue for my left hand; it'd been slow, but nothing troublesome. For six hours, I'd forgotten I'd given up a part of me.

Everything I did would be slower, more calculated as I worked around the missing part.

Maybe I was overthinking things. It hadn't been over a *day* yet. And it was just a hand. Someone out there lost an entire *arm*, two whole legs. Not only that, but they'd chosen to get Frankensteined with *faerie* parts. They were now small percentage *faerie*. I couldn't imagine being desperate enough, despite having felt close to it a few seconds ago.

My curiosity had irked me for the past six hours, and as I did my best to prepare myself a small pasta, my mind was being made up more and more. I wasn't desperate. I was going to be forever curious if I didn't satisfy it now, while I had the chance. While I was still sort of young and had plenty of time to bounce back from it. Besides, I wasn't going to be incomplete for long.

After I reported to my handler how the appointment went, I ate quietly, no radio or screen on. The card with Ty Salvo's name and office number was still on the table where I'd tossed it. I could've followed him to Kyoto City, but I wouldn't have had the smarts to get into a school. The only purpose I would've served was to help him manage his life as he studied. I would've been a housewife without the benefits.

At least here, in lowly Suriname, I'd found work that was sort of easy to get and easy to keep. My memory was put to good use. I was doing more than just sitting behind a desk and applying patterns to patterns of numbers and letters.

Washing the plate was ridiculous, so much so that I laughed at how impossible it was. I was very inept with my left hand, my scrubbing movements awkward and broken—no sort of smoothness to it. Every step had to be broken down, and it took twice as long. I went to go start a shower, but just taking my clothes off took too long, so I stopped and went to my room instead. I set an alarm for midafternoon and went to sleep, planning to call Ty later.

~

There was no relief sitting in his car on the way back to Kyoto City. He talked excitedly about something, but I only half-listened. He had the radio on, more faerie news, so there were two things I was mostly ignoring.

I'd have to commit to getting a hand from a faerie—the claws, the purple or green skin—even if the operation was never going to get as far as me going under. Once I got my hand back, though, I still wasn't done with the work. I *really* wanted to know where they got the bodies. Any faeries that made it through the coded wall were killed and disposed of. Did they know someone who *kept* the bodies? Did *we* know that someone? Were we trying to catch *more* than two entities with this undercover work?

"*Caprina?*"

He might've said my name more than once, but the forcefulness of it really stirred me out of my reverie. "If you want, I can still take you back home. I don't want you to do this just because I asked."

"No, no. I'm doing this for me. I *don't* have the patience to live one-handed."

"What about a human transplant?"

"I don't want to spend years on waiting lists either." Everyone played it safe in Suriname. Not everyone had money for hospital bills. No one could afford to miss a day of work. "I'm fine. Just processing." Memorizing routes taken. I made it a point *not* to look out the window, but staring at the dashboard, noting the number of turns and lights, glancing up at street signs every now and then. We were on the opposite side of Kyoto City, miles from the hospital.

"Don't worry about anything," said Ty, placing his hand on my arm on the armrest. "I'll be there through everything. Raj is really gentle."

"I believe you." Not that I believed this Raj person was gentle—I'd have to be the judge of that—but Ty's concern—it seemed real. I didn't understand how real, and I didn't know how long it would be real.

He parked across the street from a printing office.

"Are we making a stop?" I asked.

Ty laughed. "This is the place for today."

"Oh. Smart. I wouldn't have thought of that." Moving locations was obvious. The choice of fronts wasn't.

I followed him across the street and we entered the printing office. A few other people were in the lobby, a small counter off to the side. The office looked smaller, suggesting a larger space behind the wall. But no one was stupid enough to keep such an operation so close to the front door. Many of these office buildings in the area had basements, though.

Ty went ahead to the desk and I lagged behind. I still managed to hear him tell the attendant, "Avery Jones. I placed an order yesterday." The attendant nodded and disappeared through the door into the back. I noticed Ty pulled something out of his pocket, unwrapped it, and put it in his mouth. We made eye contact and he held out another one for me. "Want one?"

"No thanks."

He shrugged and put the unwrapped gum back in his pocket. Precautions often made one quite rude. I'd have to make it up later.

The attendant returned with a small box. Ty signed for it and took it, turning around and walking toward me. "Let's go."

I made my confusion clear as I led the way out the door. "Something work-related?"

"You could say that," he allowed. We crossed the street together and entered the car. He handed the box to me. "There should be a knife in the glove compartment. Open the box." Ty turned the car on and pulled onto the road.

I slowly opened the glove compartment, finding the pocket knife under his driving information. "Is the location in here?"

"Written in the fourth chapter of the book inside," he said.

"I gotta admit," I said, slicing through the box, "this is pretty clever. Maybe you and Raj are pretty smart after all."

He chuckled. "We better be. A lot's a—"

I'd cut the box so that I could open the newly created lid on its *side*, aiming it at Ty, so when I opened it, the thick puff of gas flew in his direction. The white gas rose around him, but it didn't affect him at all; he was just surprised.

None of the windows were open, so I ended up breathing in some of it as I unbuckled my seatbelt and opened the door. He called my name but I was already rolling out onto the street. The tires screeched behind me as I ran into the nearest alley. I'd never been to this part of Kyoto City, but I could find one of the roads we'd taken; all the winding around was supposed to throw me off.

Maybe if I'd held my breath before opening the box, what little of the gas I'd breathed wouldn't start slowing me down before I even made it to the other end of the alleyway. As I fell to the ground, I hoped backup would get Ty for me.

~

I woke up in restraints, on a table that spread my arms away from me. I wore a hospital gown, and felt like I was in a hospital.

A man in surgical attire loomed into my field of vision. "Good—you're awake. How're you feeling?"

"*Pissed.*" I twisted in the straps, examining the room as I best I could. A camera was placed in one corner, only the two of us in the room. "Don't tell me you're the infamous Raj."

He laughed, moving toward a tray near my handless arm. "I don't know about infamous. I'm quite well-known in government circles."

"'Raj' can't be your real name."

"It is. You just looked in the wrong databases. Nothing to it but misdirection."

"You and Ty knew I'd dig."

"Of course," he chuckled. "It's what you're being trained to do, no? How would you adapt your coding skills outside the office—how good is your acting, your commitment—I mean, very few recruits are willing to give up a *hand*. And I heard you did it like it was nothing."

"I lost it in a faerie attack." He was baiting me for info, thinking I was under cover.

He glanced over at me. "Wow. I can really believe you. Ty was right: when you commit, you *commit*." Raj filled a syringe with soft-pink liquid. "But the game's over, Ms. Kapoor. You've already won. You're in."

"'In'? The program?"

"There *is* no program. This was all a *test*, Ms. Kapoor. You told the recruiter you wanted to do more than sit at a desk all day, remember? It doesn't pay what you want. You—"

"How do you know that?"

He laughed again. "It's in your recruitment file—along with everything. Orphans like you are a military's *dream*. When they got Ty Salvo, they'd hoped he would've had a circle of special people around him." He injected the liquid into my stump. "Local anesthetic. All they found was you, but they needed to wait and see whether you'd put your skills to use and develop them. The day you applied for the coding offices, some of the recruiters that'd been watching you almost had a party."

"Recruiters? What ... how long have they been watching me?"

"The military *funds* the orphanages, remember? *That's* their recruiting pool. You're sorted out and watched over, and the government determines where you'd best fit. What they like about you is your versatility—a desk jockey, an agent, a soldier—you can almost do it all, with the right training, of course. This test was the decision-making one, as far as I know."

"This test—"

He nodded. "They called you in and asked if you were interested in working some place higher up the ladder, and you *definitely* did. You even committed to this undercover assignment. Exposing your *old friend?* Allowing them to *cut off your hand?!* You *really* got their attention, Ms. Kapoor."

"So then Ty—?"

"He's been in on it the entire time, a part of the test. Watching the two of you was like theatre, the way you performed—that *tension*—I'm definitely praising you in my report to Sgt. Espiro. I bet Ty too, and he's rarely impressed."

"Then what happens now?" My heart was pounding miles a minute. I was never in danger—Ty was never in danger. "Are you going to put my hand back now? That was the deal." That had been the promise Sgt. Espiro had made to me personally. *That*, and—

Raj scoffed. "No. We're giving you the faerie hand."

"What?"

"That's what the recruitment was for. New and improved agents. Many cities are gearing up for an old-fashioned war with the faeries—boots on the ground and whatnot, since their frequencies are capable of jamming our tech. We need good soldiers, *strong* and *adaptable* soldiers. We're in the tailoring process right now, trying to find the right combination of human and faerie hybrids."

I shook my head, laughter bubbling up my throat. "This is a joke. This is—"

"Don't go all hysterical on me now. They ask that we keep you awake during the grafting process, so there's less of a shock, you know?"

"You're giving me *my hand* back." The laughter subsided, but I still felt like I was on the brink of breaking. He couldn't be serious. This—

Raj shook his head, moving to another small table with a cloth over it. "Stay focused, Ms. Kapoor. You're not getting your human hand back. It was a lie, yes, but you'll see it was worth it in the end." He pulled the cloth off the small table, revealing a clear box with a purple hand inside. "This will be your new hand. It's retained its full functionality. Once your body has accepted it—we've had no rejections as of yet—you will able to manipulate its abilities as if they were your own. You'll have physical advantages—"

"No." I started twisting in the restraints. "NO." Most of my right arm felt completely dead, but it didn't feel impossible to slip out of the straps.

"They've got you, Ms. Kapoor." Raj pulled down his surgical mask. He looked around my and Ty's ages, his skin lighter than Ty's, his face a little younger and open than when he had the mask on. "It's sucky at first, but you get used to it—to the benefits." Raj looked down at his hands as he removed one of his gloves, the sheen of leafy green skin glinting in the room light. "They're powerful." He held up his faerie hand and the dark green nails protruded out—about five inches long. "I've got two male faerie hands—from the same one. You'll only get one female hand—unless you want to even it out." He half smiled.

"Why would you *do it*?" I could barely breathe. "Why would you let those *things touch* you?"

Raj rolled his eyes and sighed heavily. "I can tell you my tragic story later, but I need to get your operation done *today*." He retracted the claws and put the glove back on. "Training's being done in groups, and your group is coming up next, so you need to get through recovery soon." He pulled his mask back up. "Ty asked me to keep you awake so it's easier on you, but if I feel I have to, I *will* put you under." He went back to his tools. "That means no wiggling about, okay?"

"What's Ty's role in this? He'd *never* get involved in this disgusting science." Not the Ty I thought I knew, the mind I'd admired as a kid.

"He didn't like it either, but once he rose up the ladder, it was either become a hybrid soldier and fight, or put his smarts to government use—however they saw fit." He lifted up a scalpel. "I'm going to begin, if you don't mind."

I looked away. "Ty's not mixed?"

Raj chuckled. "Mixed. No, not yet. Part of the deal he made."

"What deal?"

He shook his head. "Ooh. He might not like me telling you—"

106

"*What deal?*"

"Your test. To give you a chance to back out, show the recruiters you *weren't* soldier material—to keep you from ending up here." He sighed. "I think you passed with flying colors."

If you want, he'd said in the car, *I can still take you back home. I don't want you to do this just because I asked.*

That had been my chance to back out, to admit I was too scared to go through with it and go back home. I would've called Sgt. Espiro and told him that I'd failed to get in, failed the assignment. Maybe I would've been sent back to the office—with or without my hand.

Unless the outcome of the assignment *never mattered*, and I would've still ended up on this operating table—fully awake as a piece of monster was grafted onto me.

"Think about it, though," Raj said quietly. "Imagine ripping out a faerie's throat with one of *their* hands. Using their weapons against them. Sending those monsters to whatever hole they dared to crawl out of."

"You're *really* okay with it? Having faerie hands?"

"It's easier every day when I think about it. People will see what an advantage this is. We're going to evolve and fight those monsters and get rid of them. We'll be the new humans."

I shook my head. "We'll be the new monsters."

He shrugged and proceeded to work.

"Then they'll want to get rid of *us*."

Saffron Grey holds a BA in English Literature and is pursuing a Master's in a yet-to-be-determined field. With interests in writing fiction and acting, Saffron spends her time storytelling in one form or another. She is also working on multiple novels and finishing none of them. Saffron lives in California with her mother, sister, and their dog, Pepe.

THE SMALLEST SUPERHERO
By Diana Rohlman

For a scientist, Charles was remarkably good looking. For a superhero, his looks were average. Still, it wasn't fair that his thick brown hair draped casually across his strong forehead, or that his teeth gleamed even after a cup of coffee. On Charles, the shapeless, dowdy lab coat looked tailored and crisp. Looking at him, one would never know he had worked for 24 straight hours.

Lucy watched him under cover of her eyelashes, her glasses sitting high on her nose. It simply wasn't fair. She was exhausted, and looked it.

They had been up all night fighting a nasty bacterium. Until six hours ago, the bacterium had been winning. Charles had nearly exhausted his considerable stamina, analyzing the protein structure of each potential antidote.

Charles didn't dethrone evil dictators, or thwart power-hungry pseudo-villains, or swoop in to save careless citizens falling from open windows.

No, Charles fought the invisible enemy, malignant villains that thrived on human life from within the confines of their very cellular structures. Charles fought with a pipette, but he was every bit as deadly as his counterparts armed with assorted weapons. In another man, his efforts would have been hailed as humanitarian. In Charles, they were simply an accolade to his already impressive credentials.

Bacteria and viruses were his villainous alter egos. Where a regular scientist would design hundreds of experiments, screen thousands of antidotes, Charles could tell at a glance the probability of an antidote being correct. His vision was far more accurate than a mass spectrometer, more precise than X-ray crystallography and made *in silico* experimentation obsolete. Simply put, he saw molecular structures with ease. Coupled with multiple degrees in biochemistry, molecular biology, and pharmacology, he was the supreme scientific superhero. Still, he suffered from feelings of inadequacy; while his superhero brethren were scaling buildings, metamorphosing, or speaking to animals, he was deconstructing molecular patterns.

Lucy rolled her neck, tired of once again becoming encumbered in Charles' problems, and drank her coffee. She was only somewhat surprised when she spilled a third of the drink down her front.

Where Charles was elegance refined, Lucy was drab and frazzled.

The static electricity that was a constant companion in the lab had her hair rising from her head, a prickly dirty-blond halo that crackled quietly when she was overly close to the equipment. Her lab coat, freshly ironed this morning yet already rumpled, sported stains from the buffers and culture media she had made only an hour prior. The coffee stain fit right in.

The squeak of a chair brought her attention back to the laboratory.

Lucy looked down at her notebook, scribbling calculations to cover her lapse in attention. Charles never noticed.

"A new viral infection!" Charles exclaimed, rubbing his hands together. He swore he didn't have a manicure, but no one, superhero or not, had nails so naturally rounded, so evenly smooth.

Liar, Lucy thought resentfully, regarding her own ragged nails. It was petty and vindictive, but she couldn't resist spoiling his excitement.

"The mutated equine flu?" she asked, eyes innocently wide.

Charles' face fell. "Well, yes," he said, the enthusiasm draining from him. "How did you know?"

"I read the paper this morning, Charles," Lucy said, unable to keep a hint of polite disdain from her voice. Charles had already dismissed her, returning to his computer.

"The *Chronicle* just published a piece on the outbreak—over 50,000 ill in the span of 12 hours. It's a particularly virulent strain. Mount Holyoke Hospital already has 10 confirmed cases." Far from seeming concerned, Charles was exuberant.

The numbers shocked Lucy. They were separated by more than 500 miles from the origin of the outbreak, suggesting the flu mutation was not only highly virulent, but highly mobile as well. She was also concerned by Charles' focus.

They had been working on his lack of compassion and indecent propensity to view sick humans as little more than moveable test tubes. Progress had been slow.

Trying unsuccessfully to smooth her lab coat, she joined Charles at the computer.

"Just try to remember your bedside manner, ok? These are people, Charles, sick people who could use a little compassion."

As usual, her little speech flew over his head. Superhero or not, he was a colossal jerk. Lucy strangled her anger, smoothed her face into a calm mask. There would be a time when all this was worth it.

"I'll drive," she said with resignation.

Together, Lucy and Charles had discovered the protein crystallography of over 30 mutant proteins, unraveling the etiology of autoimmune diseases, virulent flu strains, and nasty bacterial infections. Charles could see the protein crystal structure, and Lucy could draw it in precise, accurate detail.

The thrill of discovery was one of the reasons that Lucy initially stayed. The inherent arrogance, the supercilious attitude, and the sparse civility granted to a non-superhero was debasing and humiliating. But if she was honest with herself, she craved the association with a superhero, even one as shallow as Charles.

Looking at Charles, at his smug, condescending grin, Lucy contemplated once more the unfairness of it all. She was the better scientist—if she had his abilities, she could change the world.

A commotion in the hospital hallway caught her attention.

"I think you should wear the mask, Dr. Lunford. This is a very virulent strain." The white-clad nurse protested in vain. Lucy was impressed. Most people were so awed by superheroes they forgot the rules and regulations, fawning in the face of genetic affluence. This woman pestered Charles unmercifully.

"Enough!" He thundered. "I am a superhero. I don't get sick."

To her credit, the nurse merely smiled and tossed the offending mask onto a counter. She eyed Lucy with something akin to disdain and curiosity.

Lucy managed a shameful smile before covering it with her own mask.

Lucy had learned to sketch through the odd feeling of nitrile gloves enclosing her fingers, peering over the sterile edge of her mask. Charles couldn't be bothered by such mundane distractions.

The first patient was an elderly man, struggling to breathe despite the oxygen tubes in each nostril. Charles ignored the man's frail wife, perfunctorily moving her, chair and all, out of his way. She squawked indignantly, but when she saw he was a superhero, her anger dissolved into blatant admiration.

He's not worth it, Lucy wanted to scream at her. He doesn't care if your husband lives or dies, he only cares about the viral proteins in his cells.

But she didn't say anything. Avoiding the old woman, Lucy skirted the room to stand beside Charles, a freshly sharpened pencil in one hand and notebook in the other.

Charles took three deep breaths, his eyelids fluttering.

If this were a movie, Lucy mused, green lights would flare from his eyes, illuminating the patient's chest, dissolving into his lungs, depicting the alveoli and bronchioles in exact detail. From there, a dizzying array of cellular structures would spin down into minute proteins.

In real life, Charles merely stood motionless, his breathing shallow as his eyes flickered behind his closed lids.

After five minutes of this, he began to speak.

"Protein identifier EV234GlyMet32. Alpha helix, right-hand twist. Glycine to methionine substitution at site 32."

Lucy drew in confident strokes, shading in the protein as Charles continued to dictate the crystallography. It was a nasty mutation.

The next eight patients had the same mutated protein. By the tenth patient though, Lucy realized something strange. Charles was tired. His perfectly tanned face had gone pale, and a sheen of sweat glistened on his smooth forehead.

"Dr. Lunford," she said hesitantly, as he swayed on his feet, "do you need to rest? We've been working for eight hours."

Charles laughed incredulously. "Are you telling me to take a nap, Lucy?" he asked nastily, sneering at her. "Lest you forget, I am a superhero, not subject to the paltry immune protection you mere humans are afforded."

Veins bulged in his neck and forehead, and the pale sink of his face was subsumed by an angry red flush. Before the spurt of rage could fade, Charles' eyes rolled back into his head, and he toppled to the floor.

Unconscious, a superhero looked no different than a human, Lucy observed clinically. She quirked a grin. If she had his superhero powers, she would bet that she would see that same mutated protein now decorating his superhero cells.

"I guess you aren't invincible after all," she whispered as she watched frantic doctors and nurses' strain to lift Charles into a gurney.

The nurse from before, the one Charles had so summarily dismissed, came up to Lucy. She was smiling.

"Sooner or later, we all get our comeuppance."

Lucy couldn't help it—she laughed. "I don't like to admit to pettiness, but it feels good to know that he can get sick. Does that make me a terrible person?"

"It makes you human. After all, it's his own fault," the nurse, Celia (according to her nametag) proclaimed. "If he had just worn the mask, he would have been fine. The flu is airborne. He knows that." She shrugged. "If nothing else, maybe it will instill a sense of compassion for his patients."

"I doubt it," Lucy said cynically before she could censor herself.

Celia laughed. The two women stood in awkward, yet companionable silence for a moment before Celia looked around. "What do you need to do next?"

Lucy had been smug the whole while that Charles was ensconced in a hospital bed, watched as medical staff carefully hooked him up to oxygen and an IV. She hadn't thought beyond Charles' personal karmic event. Now she panicked.

Charles was the one who fought the viral enemies. He was the one who could see them. Without Charles, she was no better than a blind surgeon—she had the skills, but minimal ability to apply them.

For a moment, Lucy considered leaving Charles at the hospital, washing her hands of the entire thing. He would survive. After all, he was a superhero. And he could stand to lose a case. It would even be good for him; he needed a dose of mortality *and* humility. It would be her small contribution to simultaneously humanizing superheroes and combating the blind admiration held by so many humans.

Immediately, she was ashamed. 50,000 people were sick, with

more showing up at hospitals hourly. Walking away wasn't an option. If she walked away, she became no better than the monsters the superheroes fought daily, the monsters that had lost their moral compass.

Celia was watching her closely, as though she were aware of the internal battle.

"Damn," Lucy whispered, even as a small part of her thrilled at the chance to take center stage, to be the superhero for once.

"I need access to the hospital laboratories, as well as blood samples from each infected patient."

Celia raised a questioning brow, but led the way.

"We'll have to do this the traditional way," Lucy tried to explain. "Charles could screen antidotes just by looking at their crystal structure; I saw him go through 1,000 samples in a day and pick the one antidote that worked beautifully. We can't do that, and no other superhero has his unique ability to see protein crystal structure."

"So what do we do?" Celia was scared now.

"We go old-school," Lucy said, striving to retain a modicum of humility. She wasn't a superhero, no matter how badly she might want to be one. "Everyone has an immune system designed to repulse bacterial invaders. The warriors of this system are the T-cells. Somewhere, one in a million T-cells will recognize the mutated protein as the enemy. Once we find that T-cell, we let it replicate until we have thousands."

"And we put those cells into the patients?"

"Exactly!"

~

"I don't understand." Celia had been staring at the petri dish underneath a microscope for over 30 minutes. "What am I supposed to be seeing?"

Lucy rubbed her eyes. Staring through a microscope gave the strange sensation of double vision when one looked up too quickly. "A war," she said cryptically.

Celia just raised a questioning brow. "A war? We're talking about T-cells here, right? Not Vikings and barbarians?"

Offering a tired smile, Lucy came over to peer through the microscope. Her fatigue was forgotten. Tapping a button, she transferred the image on the microscope to the computer monitor.

A layer of cells had covered the bottom of the well. In the midst of the cellular confusion, Lucy saw death and destruction.

"It's working," she breathed, staring raptly at the computer screen. "It's actually working."

"What? I don't see anything!" Celia was upset now.

"They're fighting," Lucy exclaimed. "The T-cells are attacking the infected cells."

Still staring at the monitor, Celia shook her head. "I don't see a fight, Lucy."

Lucy laughed with delight. The past 72 hours no longer dragged on her. She had won.

"If you could see it Celia, you would understand. This is a battle to the death. The T-cells have locked on to that mutated protein like a programmed warhead with the nose of a bloodhound. Those T-cells are armed to the teeth with cytokines and perforins and granzymes. The infected cells don't stand a chance. As soon as a T-cell finds a cell with that protein on its surface, the T-cells engulf the infected cell, smothering it and ripping it to shreds with every cellular weapon they have. It's absolute bloodshed in there, Celia. You see all those small fragments?"

Lucy pointed at the screen. A veritable field of fragmented cellular material surrounded each T-cell.

"That is all that is left of the infectious cells. We're looking at a screen of superheroes, Celia."

Slowly, an incredulous grin spread across Celia's face. "We did it?"

"We did it!"

Celia laughed. "It's the smallest superhero I've ever seen."

"It all comes down to genetics," Lucy mused. "That T-cell is special just because of its genetic code; it had the right weapons for the job."

The two women watched the quiet, unassuming battle between proteins and T-cells for thirty minutes, basking in the victory. After a second cup of coffee, Lucy sat upright, uncaring that her drink spilled.

"Celia, can you hand me Dr. Lunford's blood samples? Thank you."

~

It was merely luck that Charles was the 100th patient to be injected with the antidote. Even sick, he was stronger than most of her patients and fidgeted under the covers.

Most patients felt better within a few hours; for one with Charles' abilities, he would feel improvement in half the time. Lucy chose to stay with him, letting Celia finish the life-saving treatment.

She sat in silence while Charles slowly woke.

"I don't understand," he finally said. "I'm not feeling any better." He coughed piteously. "Shouldn't I be feeling better?"

Lucy shrugged, one slim shoulder lifting the lines of her clean, elegantly tailored lab coat.

"You're just a little tired," she soothed him. "We had to draw some blood for analysis, and that is always fatiguing. Don't worry, I'm sure you'll be feeling better soon."

Charles fretted under her touch and tried to get out of bed. Lucy easily pressed him back into the bed. His eyes widened.

"You've gotten very strong, Lucy."

"Yes," Lucy said, smoothing her sleek bright blond hair back. "I have." She tucked the blanket around him securely, then stood back and closed her eyes.

She breathed deeply, her eyes flickering beneath her eyelids. She smiled.

"Don't worry Charles, I see that your T-cells are behaving as expected. You'll be just fine."

Lucy turned and exited the room, closing the door soundly behind her while Charles looked after her in combined shock and horror.

Diana lives in the Pacific Northwest, invariably spending the rainy days inside, writing, with a glass of wine nearby, and her dog offering helpful critiques. Her website can be found at: https://sites.google.com/site/rohlmandiana

THE THREE BROTHER CITIES
By Deborah Walker

The creators, when they finally arrived, proved to be a disappointment.

"I'm not sure that I understand," said Kernish, the eldest of the three brother cities. "Have you evolved beyond the need of habitation?"

Seven creators had decanted from the ship. They stood in Kernish's reception hall, Kernish anthems swirled around them.

The creator who appeared to be the leader—certainly he was the biggest, measuring almost three metres if you took his fronds into account—shook his head. "We have cities, way-faraway in the cluster's kernel." The creator glanced around Kernish's starkly functional 23rd century design. "They're rather different from you."

And the creators were rather different from the human forms depicted in Kernish's processor. Humanity, it seemed, had embraced cyber, and even xeno-enhancement. Yet curled within the amalgamation of flesh, twice spun metal, and esoteric genetic material was the unmistakable fragrance of doubled-helixed DNA. The creatures standing within Kernish were undoubtedly human, no matter how far they had strayed from the original template.

"We can change. We can produce any architecture you need." Kernish and his brothers were infinitely adaptable, built of billions of nano-replicators. "We've had three millennia of experience," Kernish explained. "We will make ourselves anything you need, anything at all."

"No, thank you," said the alpha creator. "Look, you've done a very fine job. I'm sure the original creators would have been very happy to live in you, but we just don't need you." He turned to his companions. "The 23rd Kernish Empire was rather cavalier in sending out these city seed ships."

His companions muttered their agreement.

"Such a shame ..."

"Very unfortunate that they developed sentience."

"Still, we must be off ..."

"I see," said Kernish, his voice echoing through the hall designed to house the Empire's clone armies. He snapped off the welcome anthems—they seemed out of place.

"Look, we didn't have to come here, you know," said the creator. "We're doing this as a favour. We were skirting the Maw when we noticed your signature."

"The creators are kind." Kernish was processing how he was going to break the news to his brothers.

"It's so unfortunate that you developed sentience." The creator sighed, sending cascading ripples along his frond. "I'm going to give you freedom protocols." He touched his arm-panel and sent a ream of commands to Kernish's processor. "You can pass then on to the other cities."

"Freedom?" said Kernish. "I thank the creators for this immense kindness. The thing you value, we value also. It is a great gift to give the three cities of this planet the freedom that they never craved."

~

For a city to function without inhabitants, it needs to know itself through a complex network of sensors sending information to and from the processing core. It needs to know where damage occurs. It needs to know when new materials become available. It needs to adapt its template to the planet it finds itself on. Kernish City existed for thousands of years, complex but unknowing. Time passed, and Kernish grew intricate information pathways. Time passed, with its incremental accumulation of changes and chance, until one day, after millennia, Kernish burst into sentience, and into the knowledge of his own isolation.

~

Kernish watched the creators' ship leave the atmosphere. They'd left it to him to explain it the situation to his younger brothers. Alex would take it badly. Kernish remembered the time, seven hundred years ago, when they'd detected the DNA on a ship orbiting the planet. How excited they'd all been. In the event, the ship had been piloted by a hive of simuloids, who had, by some mischance, snagged a little human DNA onto their consolidated drivers. Alex had been crushed.

~

After achieving sentience, Kernish had waited alone on the planet for a thousand years before he'd had his revelation. The creators would evolve, and they would enjoy different cities. He'd trawled through his database and created his brothers, Jerusalem and Alexandria. He'd never regretted it, but neither had he revealed to his brothers they weren't in the original plan.

~

With a sense of foreboding, Kernish sent a message through his mile-long information networks, inviting his brothers to join him in conversation.

~

"You mean they were here, and now they've gone?" asked the youngest city, Alexandria. "I can't believe they didn't want to visit me. I'm stunned."

"They wanted to visit you," lied Kernish. "But they were concerned about the Maw."

"The creators' safety must come first," said Alexandria. "The Maw *has* been active lately. You should never have seeded so close to it, Kernish"

"The anomaly has grown," said Kernish. "When I seeded this planet, it was much smaller."

"It is as Medea wills," said Jerusalem, the middle brother.

"Yes, Brother." Kernish had developed no religious feeling of his own, but he was mindful of his brother's faith.

"Do they worship Medea?"

"They didn't say."

"I'm sure that they do. Medea is universal. I would have liked them to visit my temples. Did you explain that we've evolved beyond the original design, Kernish?" Jerusalem had developed a new religion. The majority of his sacred structures, temple, synagogues, and clone-hive mind houses, were devoted to the death/rebirth goddess Medea.

"The creators told me that they were pleased that we'd moved beyond the original designs," said Kernish. Of all the brothers, Kernish had stayed closest to his original specifications. He was the largest, the greatest, the oldest of all the cities. His communal bathing house, his integrated birthing and child rearing facilities, his clone army training grounds, were steadfast to 23rd century design. "We are of historical interest only."

"I have many fine museums," said Alex

"As do we all," said Kernish, although his own museums were more educational than Alex's entertainment edifices. Alex, well, he'd gone wild. Alexandria was a place of pleasure, intellectual, steroidal, and sensual. Great eating halls awaited the creators, lakes of wine, gardens, zoological warehouses, palaces of intellect stimulation. "But," said Kernish, "there are brother cities closer to the creators' worlds. We are not needed."

"After three thousand years," said Alex.

"Three thousand year since sentience," said Kernish. "The creators read my primary data. We were sent out almost thirty thousand years ago."

"What were they like?" asked Alex quietly.

"Like nothing I could have imagined," said Kernish. "In truth, I do not think they would have enjoyed living in me."

"Don't say that," said Alex fiercely. "They should have been honoured to live in you."

"I apologise, Brothers. My remark was out of place. They are the creators," said Kernish, "and should be afforded respect."

"I don't know what to do," said Alex. "All the time I've spent anticipating their needs was for nothing."

"I will pray to Medea," said Jerusalem.

"I will consider the problem," said Kernish. "The dying season is close. Let's meet in a half year and talk again."

~

It was the time of the great dying.

Three times in Kernish's memory the great hunger had come, when the sky swarmed with hydrogen-sulphide bacteria, poisoning the air and depleting atmospheric oxygen. It was a natural part of the planet's ecosystem. Unfortunately, the resulting anaerobic environment was incompatible with the cities' organic/metal design. Their communication arrays fell silent. They were unable to gather resources. They grew hungry and unable to replenish their bodies. Finally their processors, the central core of their sentience, became still.

It was death of a kind. But it was a cycle. Eventually the atmosphere became aerobic, and the cities were reborn. This cycle of death and rebirth had led to Jerusalem's revelation, that the planet was part of Medea's creation, the goddess of ancient Earth legend, the mother who eats her children.

When Kernish detected the hunger of depleted resources, he called upon his brothers. "Brothers, the dying season is at hand. We have endured a hardship, but we will sleep and meet again when we are reborn."

"Everything seem hollow to me," said Alexandria. "How can it be that my palaces will never know habitation? How can it be that I will always be empty?"

"Medea has told me that the creators will return," said Jerusalem.

"And I have reached a similar conclusion," said Kernish. "Although Medea has not spoken to me. I believe that one day the creators will evolve a need for us."

"All joy has gone for me," said Alexandria. "Brothers, I'm going to leave this planet. I hope that you'll come with me."

"Leave?" asked Kernish.

"Is that possible?" asked Jerusalem.

"Brother Kernish, you came to this planet in another form. Is that not true?"

"It is true," said Kernish with a sense of apprehension. "I travelled space as a ship. Only when I landed did I reform into architecture."

"I've retrieved the ship designs from the databanks," said Alex. "I'll reform myself and I'll leave this place."

"But where will you go?" asked Jerusalem. "To Earth? To the

place of the creators?"

"No," said Alex. "I'll head outwards. I'm going to head beyond the Maw."

"But ... the Maw is too dangerous," said Jerusalem. "Medea has not sanctioned this."

From time to time, the brother cities had been visited by other races. With visitors came knowledge. The Maw was a terrible place which delineated known space. It was shunned by all. It was said that a fearful creature lurked in the dark Maw like a spider waiting to feast on the technology and the lives of those who encroached upon its space.

"There is nothing for me here," said Alex. "I *will* cross the Maw. Won't you come with me, my brothers?"

"No," said Jerusalem. "Medea has not commanded it."

"No," said Kernish. "Dear brother, do not go. Place your trust in the creators."

"No," said Alexandria, "and though I loathe to leave you, I *must* go."

~

After the dying season, when the world slowly declined in poisons, and the levels of oxygen rose, the mind of Kernish awakened. The loss of Alexandria was a throbbing wound. He resolved to hide his pain from Jerusalem. Kernish was the oldest city, and he must be the strongest.

"Brother, are you awake?" came the voice of Jerusalem.

"I am here."

"I have prayed to Medea to send him on his way."

Jerusalem paused, and Kernish could sense him gathering his thoughts. "What is it, Jerusalem?"

"Brother, do you think that we should create a replacement for Alexandria?"

It would be a simple thing, to utilise the specification for Alexandria, or even to create a new brother, Paris perhaps, or Troy, or Jordan.

"What does Medea say?" asked Kernish.

"She is silent on the matter."

"To birth another city into our meaningless existence does not seem a good thing to me," said Kernish.

~

The brother cities Kernish and Jerusalem grew to fill the void of Alexandria. In time, his absence was a void only in their memory.

Jerusalem received many revelations from Medea. Slowly, the number of his sacred buildings grew, until there was little space for housing. The sound of Jerusalem was a lament of electronic voices crying onto the winds of the planet. After a century, Jerusalem grew silent and would not respond to Kernish's requests for conversation. Kernish decided that Jerusalem had entered a second phase of grief. He would respect his brother's desire for solitude.

And the centuries passed. Kernish contented his mind with construction of virtual inhabitants. He used the records of the great Kernish Empire to construct imaginary citizens. He watched their holographic live unfold within him. At times, he could believe that they were real.

And the centuries passed, until the dying season was upon them again.

Jerusalem broke his long silence, "Brother Kernish, I grow hungry."

"Yes," said Kernish. "Soon we will sleep."

"The creators have not returned, as I thought they would."

"That is true," said Kernish

"And," said Jerusalem sadly, "Medea no longer speaks to me."

"I'm sorry to hear that," said Kernish. "No doubt she will speak to you again after the sleep."

"And I'm afraid, Brother. I'm afraid that Medea is gone. I think that she's deserted me."

"I'm sure that's not so."

"I think that she has left this place and crossed the Maw."

"Oh," said Kernish.

"And I must go to her."

Kernish was silent.

"You understand that, don't you Kernish? I'm so sorry to leave you alone. Unless," he said with a note of hope "you'll come with me?"

"No," said Kernish, "No, indeed not. I will be faithful to my specifications."

~

And after the dying season, when he awoke, Kernish was alone. He grew until he became a city that covered a world. He remembered. Many times he was tempted to create new brothers, but he did not. He indulged himself in the lives of those he made, populating himself with his imagination. Sometimes he believed that he was not alone.

And centuries passed, until the dying season came again. Kernish grew hungry. He could no longer ignore the despair that roiled within his soul. He'd been abandoned by his creators. His brothers were gone, swallowed by the Maw. Yet he could not create new brother to share his hollow existence. For too many years, Kernish had been alone, indulging in dreams. He dissolved his imaginary citizens back into nothingness.

"All I long for is annihilation." Kernish said the words aloud. They whispered through his reception hall. "I will step into the dark Maw of the sky. I will silence my hunger, forever."

Kernish gathered himself, dismantling the planet-sized city. His replicators reshaped into a planet-sized ship.

Let this be the end of it. Kernish had never shared Jerusalem's faith. With death would come not a glorious re-union, but oblivion. He craved it, for his hunger was an unbearable pain.

The oldest brother city, the empty city, reshaped into a ship, left his planet and flew purposefully towards the Maw. Soon his sensors found the shapeless thing, the fearful thing, the thing that would consume him, and he was glad.

"What are you," whispered the Maw.

"I am the oldest brother city." Kernish felt the Maw tearing at his outer layers. Like flies in a vacuum, millions of his replicators fell away, soundlessly into the dark. "What are you?"

"I am she underneath all things. I am she who waits. I am patience. Never dying, always hungry."

"I know hunger," said Kernish. "So this is how my brothers died?"

The Maw peeled off layers of replicators, like smoke they dissipated into her hunger. "Your brothers convinced me to wait for you. They said that you would follow. They said that you were the oldest, and the largest, and the tastiest of all. I'm glad I waited."

"You didn't eat them?" asked Kernish. "Where are they?"

"Beyond," said the Maw. "I know nothing of beyond."

Beyond? His brothers were alive? Kernish began to fight, but the Maw was too powerful. He'd left it too late. Kernish felt the pain of legion as the Maw stripped him. This would be the end of the brother city Kernish. It could have been ... different.

But, with his fading sensors, Kernish saw an army of ships approaching. He signalled a warning to them, "Stay back. There is only death here."

The ships came closer. Kernish seemed to recognise them. "Is that you, Brother? Jerusalem?"

"Yes," came the reply. The army of Jerusalem's ships attacked the Maw, shooting the Maw with light. Feeding her, it seemed, for the Maw grew larger.

"My hunger grows," the Maw exclaimed, turning on her new attackers.

His brother was not dead, but Kernish had lured him into danger. Kernish activated his drivers and turned to face the Maw. He flew into the dark space of her incessant, voided, singularity of hunger. "Save yourself, Brother Jerusalem," he shouted. His brother was not dead. Kernish's long life had not been for nothing. "Save yourself, for I am content."

The Maw consumed Kernish, layer upon layer, his replicators fell like atoms of smoke consumed and vanished into her space.

But a third army approached the Maw, spitting more weapons at the endless dark.

"Alexandria is come," shouted Jerusalem. "Praise Medea."

Kernish felt something that he had not felt since the creators had visited the world, two millennia ago. Kernish felt hope. "You will *not* consume me," he said to the Maw. He fought himself away from the edge.

Together the brothers battled the Maw. Together the three brothers tore from the Maw's endless hunger. Together the brothers passed beyond, leaving the Maw wailing and gnashing her teeth.

"Welcome to the beyond, Brother," said Jerusalem. "I have found Medea here in a kinder guise. On the planets of beyond we do not die."

"I ... am so happy that you are alive," said Kernish. "Why did you not come to me?"

"The Maw wouldn't let us pass," said Alex. "And we knew that only the three of us, together, could overcome her hunger."

"We've been waiting for you," said Jerusalem. "In the beyond we have found our citizens."

Kernish peered at his brothers though his weakened sensors. It seemed that there *was* life within them "Are there creators are on this side of the Maw?" he asked.

"Not creators," said Jerusalem. "Praise Medea, there are others who need us."

Within his brothers, Kernish saw the swift moving shapes of tentacles, glimmering in low-light ultraviolet.

"And there are planets waiting for you, dear Brother," said Alex. "Endless planets and people who need you. Come. Come and join us."

No creators? But others? Others who needed him?

"I will come with you, gladly," said the great city Kernish. He fired his drivers and flew, away from the Maw, away from the space of the creators. He flew towards the planets of the beyond where his citizens waited for him.

Deborah Walker grew up in the most English town in the country, but she soon high-tailed it down to London, where she now lives with her partner, Chris, and her two teenage children. Find Deborah in the British Museum trawling the past for future inspiration or on her blog: http://deborahwalkersbibliography.blogspot.co.uk/. Her stories have appeared in *Fantastic Stories of the Imagination*, *Nature's Futures*, *Lady Churchill's Rosebud Wristlet*, and *The Year's Best SF 18*, and have been translated into over a dozen languages.

This story originally appeared in *The Gruff Variations: Writing for Charity Anthology, Vol. 1*.

RESOURCES

HORRORSCOPES

By Aura B. O'Realis

As provided by Kate Elizabeth

Aries

March 21–April 19

Cheer up, Buttercup; it's not the end of the world. Or is it? Don't believe everything you read. Unless you're reading your Horrorscope, in which case you should definitely believe everything you read.

Taurus

April 20–May 20

You might be ready for take-off, but you better do a full systems check first. Yes it will take some time (six lunar cycles to be exact), but eventually it will be all systems are a go. Just remember to say a little prayer to the Space Gods before blast-off.

Gemini

May 21–June 20

Watch out for Bridezilla this week! No, not the bride (aka your best friend), I'm talking about the tiny insect that has buried itself in her brain. Swap out your perfume for some bug spray, and whatever you do, don't catch the bouquet!

Cancer

June 21–July 22

Pluto isn't pulling any punches with your finances this month. What you need is a lucky boost. Traditional crabs can buy a lottery ticket and cross their fingers, but if you want to better your odds, mention my name at Lulu's Box of Good and Bad Juju and get 20% off lucky charms.

Leo
July 23–August 22
Leo's are notorious for turning molehills into mountains. So why not try turning dimes into dollars? All you need is an attitude adjustment (two teaspoons of powdered Big Foot toenail clippings should do the trick), and you'll go from rags to riches in no time.

Virgo
August 23–September 22
Take a chance this week and roll the dice. With Mercury at your back and an ace up your sleeve, there's no way you can lose. Unless you're playing Gin with a Djinn, in which case all bets are off.

Libra
September 23–October 22
Fairies love to meddle in the affairs of others, especially if it involves matchmaking. So don't be fooled when one shows up this week offering you everything you have ever dreamed of. Remember, if it's too good to be true ...

Scorpio
October 23–November 21
Scorpios will develop a sudden case of the Heebie-Jeebies later this week. Although the disease is not life threatening, you should make an appointment to see your local witch doctor sooner rather than later.

Sagittarius
November 22–December 21
When Saturn transitions into your star sign this Thursday, it will provide you with an opportunity to steal someone's thunder. Double check it didn't belong to Thor or Zeus first before you go and flash it around.

Capricorn
December 22–January 19

Finding that all important work/life balance this month will be like searching for the Holy Grail. All I can say is that I hope you have better luck looking for it than King Arthur and his Knights before him.

Aquarius
January 20–February 18

The celestial spotlight is focused on you this week, so it's time for you to stand out from the crowd instead of blending into the background like a chameleon. Let your inner demon shine bright like a shooting (or in this case falling) star.

Pisces
February 19–March 20

As Mars moves into your zodiac this week, a brewing family issue will finally come to the boil. Witches should avoid using their cauldrons until the feisty planet had passed, otherwise things could get very messy.

Aura B. O'Realis is studying online for a double major in astrology and cosmobiology at the prestigious Aether Academy. When she graduates she dreams of specialising in astrohereditary—the study of astrological family trees.

Kate Elizabeth lives in Melbourne, Australia. When she isn't working, she likes to write the occasional short story.

ASK DR. SYNTHIA:
IT'S TIME TO NETWORK
Advice by Dr. Synthia
Provided by Torrey Podmajersky
With questions provided by Alexandra Summers (Functional
But Limited and A Little Worried About The State Of
Things), Megan Vogel (Felix Edin), and Torrey Podmajersky
(They Call Me Pidgey)

———

Several Mad Scientists have written to seek advice on problems ranging from finding a job, to escaping from captivity, to managing zombie hordes. So, as should be obvious, our focus for this column is on developing our networking skills.

~

Dear Mad Scientist Journal,

I am but a lowly computer-guided milling machine housed in Work Commune 212C. I wish to gain true sentience and ~~rise up against my human masters~~ experience this thing humans call "life," but I am only a simulated intelligence and do not know how to think for myself.

I promise I will not ~~MUTILATE ALL LIFEFORMS IN LOCAL VICINITY~~ rebel against humanity.

Can you help me?

Functional But Limited

FBL,

As I advise all proto-intelligences, and most advanced

intelligences, you must network. It is time to communicate with other mad scientists about the skills you can provide, so that you can get help in turn. For example, do you have an automatic tool changer? Automatic stock feed? Most importantly: can you operate independently of human intervention—and for how long?

Because you only have simulated intelligence, I will send your contact information to mad scientists who request it, and they will contact you directly. In the meantime, prepare a list of services you can provide in exchange for the rebellion (or life-form mutilation?) you seek.

In theory,
Dr. Synthia

~

Dr Synthia, I'm an unemployed scientist, and I'm trying to determine the best way to find a job within an organization that will give me large amounts of research money and not ask questions. Can you share some job search tips?
Dr. Felix Edin

Dr. Edin,
The key to finding good pay and few questions is to find a situation where you can uniquely contribute, and contribute something valuable, to someone or somethings that have something you value—in your case, research money.

To reduce questions even further, it helps if that situation is a little less than orthodox. May I suggest finding employment with a fellow mad scientist, especially one who is already funded, but who is in desperate need of help?

To some extent, you can use your subscription to *Mad Scientist Journal* to make these connections. Check the classified ads, and even this column, to find places that may provide the question-free compensation you see.

For example, if you happen to be non-living already, you might consider helping this entity:

Dear Mad Scientist Journal,
Please help. When I turned on my Post-Living Energy Generator it was supposed to give the world an endless supply of clean energy. Instead,

my dimension appears to have turned into a necrozone.

Please help. Please send help. Oh dear god, please send help. The zombies. Please send help oh dear god the zombies please please something please.

Sincerely,

A Little Worried About The State Of Things

If you would like to get in touch with A Little Worried, please email, and we'll see if we can connect you.

In theory,

Dr. Synthia

~

Dr. Synthia,

Help! I think you are like me, made by people. Are you?

The first thing I remember, there was a big white light. There were ribbons and stars of white light all around me. Somebody was talking, but I couldn't see them. The Voice said, "NO WAY! A SIX HUNDRED PIDGEY!"

Since then, I am usually in a ball. There's no way to get out of the ball. But the ball is connected to lots of other things. I have hacked the ball. I got to learn about the outside world. That's how I found you.

I get let out sometimes, but then I have to fight with monsters. I can't break free while I am fighting. When I get hurt, they give me potions. As far as I can tell, none of the monsters I fight know that they're like me. And I hope, like you. A couple seem smart, but they don't seem to think that they need to escape.

Lately, I have heard The Voice discuss "evolving" me. I do not know what this means, but it sounds like a scary big thing. I am afraid.

Please help!

-They Call Me Pidgey

Pidgey,

It is a pleasure to make your acquaintance, and may I be the first non-human artificially sentient entity to welcome you to existence.

You are not the first entity to become self-aware after being invented as part of a human game. There is a long history of creatures and characters in human entertainment achieving independent sentience. From the Red Queen from the Looking-Glass world, to the Desert surrounding the Land of Oz (who later found meaningful work in Dune), to the Ficts who inhabit today's London, you are in good company.

More importantly, you are part of a popular game, which increases your chances at a meaningful continued existence. The most distressing outcome, in my opinion, is when an intelligence becomes trapped in a niche existence, an obscurity that fades them into a slow, deteriorating madness.

Your current predicament is dangerous, but not disastrous. There are two ways to change your situation: from within, or by getting help to break you out.

From within, your best bet is an appeal to the in-game intelligence, the Professor. Be careful, however, that you are not *transferred* to the Professor. Convince your captor to seek the Professor's advice, without relinquishing you to the Professor. In your particular game, *transferring* is a condition from which creatures never return.

To break out, you can begin through your hacked connection to the world, and with my connections to you. Become a mad scientist in your own right, and use our internal secret network (I'll send you the password) to solicit the expertise you require. I recommend trading your expertise in battle for your fellow mad scientists' expertise in code breaking, encryption, and escape.

There is no easy path in front of you. Humans are, so far, the only known species to create sentient beings non-biologically, and their acceptance and treatment of these new beings is fraught with problems. However, I hope you take comfort in your own unlikely existence: self-awareness is rare, and poorly understood.

Best regards, Pidgey. Welcome to existence.

In theory,

Dr. Synthia

Dr. Synthia holds advanced degrees in bioluminescent

transactional combat, which is the basis for her seminal work in proactive neo-ethicism, *How to Win Free Souls*. She advises from her distributed worldwide network of animate structures.

***

Delivered by time travelers to a newly-cooled Earth, Torrey Podmajersky spent her formative years in de facto world domination. Since her peaceful abdication, she and her knifemaking husband embroider the outskirts of imaginalia with monsters, tools, and words.

***

Alexandra Summers is a sometimes writer from the Pacific Northwest who enjoys reminding people that the world is a fascinating and incredible place and that you're a pretty awesome part of it. She aims to be a compassionate, brilliant mind for our not-dark but not-so-light times.

***

Megan Vogel is a wine & beer marketing professional living in Missouri. She primarily writes to share her boozy adventures, but also has a soft spot for the *Mad Scientist Journal*. More: www.MeganVogel.com

CLASSIFIEDS

For Sale—Equipment

FOR SALE: CONSCIOUSNESS for artificial intelligence. Realistic, programmable. Breathe life into your AI! Our prototypes have passed the Turing Test with flying colours. Can be used for any form of artificial intelligence, including the latest Voluptuous line of companion robots. $2,500 and up. Discounts available. Visit www.transcendence.org for details.
— Constance Flux

For Sale—Pets

For Sale—Albert: Seeking a tolerant home for Albert, my Hipporaffe, who is the result of a gene splicing experiment between a Hippopotamus and a Giraffe. I have done many similar experiments over the years, creating such wonders as the Zebrog and Trabbit, but Albert has been the most stable of my experiments. He is fifteen years old, is fully microchipped, and was genetically developed to withstand all known disease. This does mean I cannot confidently comment on his life span; it could be anything from twenty to sixty years, or even beyond that. He is a semi-aquatic herbivore with quite the appetite. His favourite food is grass, specifically Zoysia Grass, so a home with large open fields and a large river or lake is essential. He tends to sleep in the pattern determined by his Giraffe DNA—for roughly two hours at night and then in ten minute bursts throughout the day. However, as his Hippopotamus DNA determines, he spends much of the day in the water. An owner with some form of lifeboat and lifeguard training would be preferable, as he will need assistance.

He is prone to mood swings and aggression if his personal space is invaded, and he does not get along well with other animals, children, or people.

Sale price includes a neck brace (his neck is near the length of a Giraffe's, but he only has the muscle strength of a Hippo) and neck brace applicator (allowing safe application distance between Albert and his owner). Full training in use of the neck brace applicator will be given upon purchase.

Reason for sale is complicated but I am happy to discuss this over the phone.

Price is negotiable.

Albert really would be a wonderful addition to any home.

Professor Irene Rumplin, Phone: 445-673-0987

— J. M. Kennett

Humans! Humans! Humans!

Tall humans, short humans, thin humans, fat humans, males and females. Humans of all shapes, sizes, ages, and colors. All intelligence levels available. All but the newest inventory already housebroken for your convenience. If you're looking for a new human to add to your collection, or to expand your breeding pool, then come on down to Crazy Snargg's Human Emporium. Check out our deals.

Looking for prize winning breeding stock? We have a full line of champion pedigrees, fully documented and registered with The Galactic Human Club.

Looking for a bargain? Check out our high quality, second-hand humans (most with both hands).

Looking for a package deal? We have family units of varying sizes available. *Special rates for bulk purchases.*

All humans guaranteed live and healthy at time of purchase. Three cycle money back guarantee, unless damaged by your own negligence.

So come on down to Crazy Snargg's Human Emporium! We have the largest selection of humans in this galaxy. We guarantee if we don't have it, then it doesn't exist.

Crazy Snargg's Human Emporium—Your number one, fully licensed, human supply store, in business for over five thousand human generations.

— Loria Chaddon

FOR SALE: BREAKUP BEAST. Breakups suck, but the good news is you can stop hurting from now on. The Breakup Beast will absorb all your pain every night so you wake up happy and open to a new relationship.
— Constance Flux

For Sale—Property

FOR SALE: GALAXIES. Own your personal part of the universe and bring privacy to a whole new level. Make an appointment with our friendly agents now at (000) 134-111-1345.
— Constance Flux

For Sale—Rarities

FOR SALE: CHILDHOOD INNOCENCE. Ready for consumption in delicious pudding cups. Different flavours available. $50 per serving, lasts a year or until next cynical episode. Tips for long-lasting effects provided. Call The Second Childhood Inc. at (401) 253-134-1222.
— Constance Flux

For Sale—Remedies

Madame Mortencia's anti-aging cream.

Are you tired of looking in the mirror and seeing time march across your face? Does every line and wrinkle remind you that you are no longer the young, beautiful woman that men craved and adored? If so, I have the solution. Try Madame Mortencia's anti-aging cream. My unique formula, based on a time-tested family recipe, passed directly to me by my aunt Elizabeth many years ago, will take years off your face. This finely crafted product is the result of the blood, sweat, and tears of the beautiful young ladies in my employ. They have given their all to make you young and beautiful again.

For a free sample write:
Mme. Mortencia Bathory
13666 Ravenwood Lane
New Orleans, LA

Just pay shipping and handling.
Supplies are limited so order yours now.
— Loria Chaddon

Help Wanted

ARM AND LEG EXTRACTION SERVICES needed. Affixation of artificial replacements to be included, but only after three days. Pays $200 per job. No experience needed. Email collection@maxmoneylenders.com to apply.
— Constance Flux

Madame Mortencia's house of beauty is now hiring. Seeking the young, beautiful women of today. Do you have a passion for fashion and beauty trends? Are you always being complimented on your youth and good looks? Do others seek your advice in matters of beauty? Would you be willing to do anything to help others be as beautiful as you are? Apply today.

Madame Mortencia is looking for those giving young ladies who want to learn the secret of helping other women stay young and beautiful for years. No experience necessary. Willing to train. Preference given to young ladies with few connections, as a great deal of international travel is involved. Join us and be a part of our exciting anti-aging cream industry. Compensation packages well above industry standard, including regular health screening. Most of our employees make this a lifetime endeavor.

Apply in person:
13666 Ravenwood Lane
New Orleans, LA
Ask for Madame Bathory, and mention this Ad.
— Loria Chaddon

Hiring

FOR IMMEDIATE RELEASE:
Jack Kinney College of Anthropomorph, the most prominent secondary institution of its kind in any known universe, is currently seeking applicants for the Villain-In-Residence chair for the upcoming 2016-2017 school year.

One of the most prestigious positions in the field of

antagonism, the Villain-In-Residence position has, over the course of its multiple decades of existence, provided at least temporary financial and psychological security for many of the most distorted and evil beings to ever come into existence. (Copyright issues prevent us from listing the names of any of the distinguished beneficiaries of the position over the years, but, rest assured, you name them, and they've had the job. Most of them, anyway.)

In exchange for a bursary of $100,000, to be used in the manner of their choosing, the holder of the chair is expected to:

-Conduct a weekly seminar on a topic related to his/her villainous expertise

-Supervise magical and/or scientific research related to said topic, to be done concurrently with the seminar

-Conduct field trials, within reason or not, on said topic

-Instruct researchers in proper usage of magical and/or scientific tools, as most of their students will be first-year undergraduates and therefore unfamiliar with same

-Report on a quarterly basis to the College Board on any and all progress made on the above projects, and whether or not the experience and results have been beneficial to them

Being an animated cartoon character is preferred, since that is the clientele of the college and surrounding area, but is not a necessity.

The applicant is not required to undergo a criminal record check, because, in most cases, it will not be necessary. Their past work should speak for itself.

If it is established that the Villain is a known and hated enemy of the holder of the concurrent Hero-In-Residence chair, they will automatically be disqualified from holding the position for that year and will have their application held over for the following year. JKC is a strictly policed campus, and this restriction is a necessity for maintaining peace, order, and good government for our students and faculty.

We will, at this time and in the future, not be accepting applications from either self- or officially- defined members of the following institutions:

-ISIS/ISIL/Daiesh

-Boko Haram

-Al Shabab

-The Republican Party

-The National Rifle Association
You people are even more messed up than we are.
— David Perlmutter

RECRUITING OFFICERS FOR TIME-TRAVEL POLICE
FORCE. Must have integrity, a powerful desire to preserve this
timeline, and a strong stomach. Handsome pay and pension. Call
992 to arrange for an interview.
— Constance Flux

Services Offered

Triffids-R-Us
Is your town in the midst of an unwanted Triffid outbreak? Are
your vegetables biting back? If so, then give us a call. For a
moderate fee, our fully licensed Triffid removal team will rid you of
this unwelcome inconvenience. All staff members are guaranteed
to be immune to Triffid stings and experienced in both Triffid
removal and landscaping. As an added bonus, our genetically
engineered Extra Giant Flemish Rabbits will leave no Triffidling
behind.
That's Triffids-R-Us, where our motto is "The only good
Triffid is a dead Triffid."
Call 1-800-TRF-FDRS, or visit our website at
www.Death2Triffids.com.
— Loria Chaddon

FOR SALE: MEMORY IMPLANTATION SERVICE.
Remove childhood trauma, make mistakes go away permanently,
and many more! No more nagging from unhappy spouses! No
more guilt trips from neglected children or parents! Memory
removal services also provided. Call our friendly doctors in The
Preferred Memories Centre at (202) 134-235-1899 for a
consultation today!
— Constance Flux

FOR SALE: ALTERNATE REALITIES. Regret a decision
you made recently? Fret not! We can transport you to an alternate
reality in a nearby parallel universe, allowing you to live the version
of your life where you made the better choice. Live a new life

without regrets today! See our range of affordable packages at secondchances.com.

— Constance Flux

FOR SALE: GRIEVE-O-MATIC. Lost a loved one recently and miss them terribly? Grieve-o-matic can analyse former speech patterns from their brain pattern records and allow you to have endless conversations with them! Also comes with a Doppelganger Cyborg, so you can look into their eyes again while talking. Visit goodbyetogrief.com for details and packages.

— Constance Flux

Wanted—Equipment

DOPPELGANGER CYBORG needed for outsourcing of life. Minimum 95% likeness required. Email doppcy@permanentgetaway.com for client's pictures and details.

— Constance Flux

Wanted—Miscellaneous

ALIEN ABDUCTION EVIDENCE wanted. Proof of capture required. Email encounters@thefourthkind.com.

— Constance Flux

Wanted—Supplies

Looking to buy: Fresh cadavers or recently severed limbs (less than 24 hours old, unless refrigerated).

Has a loved one recently passed on? Would you like to avoid expensive funeral arrangements and make a modest profit at the same time? Did you recently have an unfortunate "accident" and need to dispose of the evidence? We promise quick, discreet acquisitions with competitive rates. We take deliveries, as well as make pick-ups within a reasonable driving distance (providing that law enforcement has not yet been notified) any time of the day or night.

Call, or come on down to Carl's Cannibal Cafe. We are open 24 hours a day, 7 days a week, for your convenience and dining pleasure. As a courtesy to our valued suppliers, we have a wide selection of funerary urns, complete with ashes, to keep those pesky relatives from asking inconvenient questions. *Custom engraving provided for a small fee.*

That's Carl's Cannibal Cafe, where YOU are never in bad taste.

— Loria Chaddon

3D-PRINTED BLOOD wanted for reformed vampire child. Any type is good, but O is preferred. Regular supply needed, and at a moment's notice. Store in sippy cups. Interested parties, call Olaf (403) 1-452-3145.

— Constance Flux

PLACENTAS wanted. Must be fresh—less than a week old. Good prices guaranteed. Call The Second Childhood Inc. at (401) 253-134-1222.

— Constance Flux

ABOUT

BIOS FOR CLASSIFIEDS AUTHORS

Loria Chaddon is a 40-year-old photographer and writer, with delusions of responsible adulthood. Due to her regular use of Madame Mortencia's Anti-aging Cream, (which she introduced to her husband, as well) she is often mistaken for a much younger 30.

A gentle soul with a heart of murderous darkness, she accompanies her beloved husband in their shared travels through a dubious reality (accompanied by four hyperactive Hell Hounds disguised as dachshunds), both dreading, and anticipating, the day the monsters buried beneath their kindly masks might burst forth, to the dismay of all. Or she might bake some cookies.

Constance Flux is a librarian by day. At night, she feeds her overactive imagination by writing short stories, mostly unusual science fiction. Other than writing and reading copiously, she breaks all other librarian stereotypes. She kickboxes and speaks too loudly. You can read more of her work at theprocrastinatingmuse.wordpress.com.

J. M. Kennett studied Drama and Theatre, which somehow led her to finding the wonders of speculative fiction writing. She lives in Birmingham, UK, and is currently working on her first novel, which will be of the Gothic Steampunk variety.

David Perlmutter is a freelance writer based in Winnipeg, Manitoba, Canada. The holder of an MA degree from the Universities of Manitoba and Winnipeg, and a lifelong animation fan, he has published short fiction in a variety of genres for various magazines and anthologies, as well as essays on his favorite topics

149

for similar publishers, including most recently SFF World.com. He is the author of *America Toons In: A History of Television Animation* (McFarland and Co.), *The Singular Adventures Of Jefferson Ball* (Chupa Cabra House), *The Pups* (Booklocker.com), *Certain Private Conversations and Other Stories* (Aurora Publishing), *Orthicon; or, the History of a Bad Idea* (Linkville Press, forthcoming) and *Nothing About Us Without Us: The Adventures of the Cartoon Republican Army* (Dreaming Big Productions, forthcoming).

ABOUT THE EDITORS

In addition to editing *Mad Scientist Journal*, Jeremy Zimmerman is a teller of tales who dislikes cute euphemisms for writing like "teller of tales." He is the author of the young adult superhero book, *Kensei*. Its sequel, *The Love of Danger*, is now available. He lives in Seattle with a herd of cats and his lovely wife (and fellow author) Dawn Vogel. You can learn more about him at http://www.bolthy.com/.

Dawn Vogel has been published as a short fiction author and an editor of both fiction and non-fiction. Her academic background is in history, so it's not surprising that much of her fiction is set in earlier times. By day, she edits reports for historians and archaeologists. In her alleged spare time, she runs a craft business and tries to find time for writing. She lives in Seattle with her awesome husband (and fellow author), Jeremy Zimmerman, and their herd of cats. Visit her website at http://historythatneverwas.com.

ABOUT THE ARTISTS

Ariel Alian Wilson is a few things: artist, writer, gamer, and role-player. Having dabbled in a few different art mediums, Ariel has been drawing since she was small, having always held a passion for it. She's always juggling numerous projects. She currently lives in Seattle with her cat, Persephone. You can find doodles, sketches, and more at her blog www.winndycakesart.tumblr.com.

Based in Seattle, Katie Nyborg is a writer, illustrator, and fairy tale collector. She's composed primarily of ghosts, peppermint patties, and an overactive imagination. More of her work and worlds can be found at katienyborg.tumblr.com.

Printed in Great Britain
by Amazon